Since its original publication in 1940, LASSIE
COME-HOME has sold more than a million
copies in the English language and has been
translated into twenty-four foreign languages. This
new paperback edition contains the author's
changes and corrections as they appear in the
Thirtieth Anniversary hardcover edition.

Born in England, ERIC KNIGHT came to Philadelphia in 1912 and worked there as a newspaperman for many years. In 1939 he moved to a farm
in Pennsylvania, where he wrote *Lassie Come-
Home* and an adult novel, *This Above All*. In
1943 he was killed in a plane crash while serving
as an officer in the United States Army.

ALSO AVAILABLE IN LAUREL-LEAF BOOKS:

LASSIE
COME-HOME

ERIC KNIGHT

LAUREL-LEAF
BOOKS

LAUREL-LEAF BOOKS bring together under a single imprint outstanding works of fiction and nonfiction particularly suitable for young adult readers, both in and out of the classroom. Charles F. Reasoner, Professor Emeritus of Children's Literature and Reading, New York University, is consultant to this series.

Published by
Dell Publishing Co., Inc.
1 Dag Hammarskjold Plaza
New York, New York 10017

Laurel-Leaf Library ® TM 766734, Dell Publishing Co., Inc.

ISBN: 0-440-94651-4

RL: 5.8

Reprinted by arrangement with Holt, Rinehart & Winston, Inc.

Printed in the United States of America

January 1976

10

WFH

To Dr. Harry Jarrett
A Man Who Knows a Dog

Contents

LASSIE
COME-HOME

Not for Sale

Everyone in Greenall Bridge knew Sam Carraclough's Lassie. In fact, you might say that she was the best-known dog in the village—and for three reasons. First, because nearly every man in the village agreed she was the finest collie he had ever laid eyes on.

This was praise indeed, for Greenall Bridge is in the county of Yorkshire, and of all places in the world it is here that the dog is really king. In that bleak part of northern England the dog seems to thrive as it does nowhere else. The wind and the cold rains sweep over the flat moorlands, making the dogs rich-coated and as sturdy as the people who live there.

The people love dogs and are clever at raising them. You can go into any one of the hundreds of small mining villages in this largest of England's counties, and see, walking at the heels of humbly clad workmen, dogs of such a fine breed and aristocratic bearing as to arouse the envy of wealthier dog fanciers from other parts of the world.

And Greenall Bridge was like other Yorkshire villages. Its men knew and understood and loved dogs, and there were many perfect ones that walked at men's heels. But they all agreed that if a finer dog than Sam Carraclough's tricolor collie had ever been bred in Greenall Bridge, then it must have been long before they were born.

But there was another reason why Lassie was so well known in the village. It was because, as the women said, "You can set your clock by her."

That had begun many years before, when Lassie was a bright, harum-scarum yearling. One day Sam Carraclough's boy, Joe, had come home bubbling with excitement.

"Mother! I come out of school today, and who do you think was sitting there waiting for me? Lassie! Now how do you think she knew where I was?"

"She must have picked up thy scent, Joe. That's all I can figure out."

Whatever it was, Lassie was waiting at the school gate the next day, and the next. The weeks and the months and the years had gone past, and it had always been the same. Women glancing through the windows of their cottages, or shopkeepers standing in the doors on High Street, would see the proud black-white-and-golden-sable dog go past on a steady trot, and would say:

"Must be five minutes to four—there goes Lassie!"

Rain or shine, the dog was always there, waiting for a boy—one of dozens who would come pelting across the playground—but for the dog, the only one who mattered. Always there would be the moment of happy greeting, and then, together, the boy and the dog would go home. For four years it had always been the same.

Lassie was a well-loved figure in the daily life of the village. Almost everyone knew her. But, most of all, the people of Greenall Bridge were proud of Lassie because she stood for something that they could not have explained readily. It had something to do with their pride. And their pride had something to do with money.

Generally, when a man raised an especially fine dog, some day it would stop being a dog and instead would become something on four legs that was worth money. It was still a dog, of course, but now it was something else, too, for a rich man might hear of it, or the alert dealers or kennelmen might see it, and then they would want to buy it. While a rich man may love a dog just as truly as a poor man, and there is no difference in them in this, there is a difference between them in the way they must look at money. For the poor man sits and thinks about how much coal he will need that winter, and how many pairs of shoes will be necessary, and how much food his children ought to have to keep them sturdy—and then he will go home and say:

"Now, I had to do it, so don't plague me! We'll raise another dog some day, and ye'll all love it just as much as ye did this one."

That way, many fine dogs had gone from homes in Greenall Bridge. But not Lassie!

Why, the whole village knew that not even the Duke of Rudling had been able to buy Lassie from Sam Carraclough—the very Duke himself who lived in his great estate a mile beyond the village and who had his kennels full of fine dogs.

For three years the Duke had been trying to buy Lassie from Sam Carraclough, and Sam had merely stood his ground.

"It's no use raising your price again, Your Lordship," he would say. "It's just—well, she's not for sale for no price."

The village knew all about that. And that was why Lassie meant so much to them. She represented some sort of pride that money had not been able to take away from them.

Yet, dogs are owned by men, and men are bludgeoned by fate. And sometimes there comes a time in a man's life when fate has beaten him to the point that he must bow his head and decide to eat his pride so that his family may eat bread.

"I Never Want Another Dog"

The dog was not there! That was all Joe Carraclough knew. That day he had come out of school with the others, and had gone racing across the yard in a rush of gladness that you see at all schools, all the world over, when lessons are over for the day. Almost automatically, by a habit ingrained through hundreds of days, he had gone to the gate where Lassie always waited. And she was not there!

Joe Carraclough stood, a sturdy, pleasant-faced boy, trying to reason it out. The broad forehead over his brown eyes became wrinkled. At first, he found himself unable to realize that what his senses told him could be true.

He looked up and down the street. Perhaps Lassie was late! He knew that could not be the reason, though, for animals are not like human beings. Human beings have watches and clocks, and yet they are always finding themselves "five minutes behind time." Animals need no machines to tell time. There is something inside them that is more accurate than clocks. It is a "time sense," and it never fails them. They know, surely and truly, exactly when it is time to take part in some well-established routine of life.

Joe Carraclough knew that. He had often talked it over with his father, asking him how it was that Lassie

knew when it was time to start for the school gate.
Lassie could not be late.

Joe Carraclough stood in the early summer sunshine,
thinking of this. Suddenly a flash came into his mind.

Perhaps she had been run over!

Even as this thought brought panic to him, he was
dismissing it. Lassie was far too well trained to wander
carelessly in the streets. She always moved daintily and
surely along the pavements of the village. Then, too,
there was very little traffic of any kind in Greenall
Bridge. The main motor road went along the valley by
the river a mile away. Only a small road came up to
the village, and that became merely narrow footpaths
farther along when it reached the flat moorland.

Perhaps someone had stolen Lassie!

Yet this could hardly be true. No stranger could so
much as put a hand on Lassie unless one of the Carraclough was there to order her to submit to it. And,
moreover, she was far too well known for miles around
Greenall Bridge for anyone to dare to steal her.

But where could she be?

Joe Carraclough solved his problem as hundreds of
thousands of boys solve their problems the world over.
He ran home to tell his mother.

Down the main street he went, racing as fast as he
could. Without pausing, he went past the shops on
High Street, through the village to the little lane going
up the hillside, up the lane and through a gate, along a
garden path, and then through the cottage door, to cry
out:

"Mother? Mother—something's happened to Lassie!
She didn't meet me!"

As soon as he had said it, Joe Carraclough knew
that there was something wrong. No one in the cottage
jumped up and asked him what the matter was. No one

seemed afraid that something dire had happened to
their fine dog.

Joe noticed that. He stood with his back to the door,
waiting. His mother stood with her eyes lowered
toward the table where she was setting out the tea-time
meal. For a second she was still. Then she looked at
her husband.

Joe's father was sitting on a low stool before the fire,
his head turned toward his son. Slowly, without speaking, he turned back to the fire and stared into it intently.

"What is it, Mother?" Joe cried suddenly. "What's
wrong?"

Mrs. Carraclough set a plate on the table slowly and
then she spoke.

"Well, somebody's got to tell him," she said, as if to
the air.

Her husband made no move. She turned her head
toward her son.

"Ye might as well know it right off, Joe," she said.
"Lassie won't be waiting at school for ye no more. And
there's no use crying about it."

"Why not? What's happened to her?"

Mrs. Carraclough went to the fireplace and set the
kettle over it. She spoke without turning.

"Because she's sold. That's why not."

"Sold!" the boy echoed, his voice high. "Sold! What
did ye sell her for—Lassie—what did ye sell her for?"

His mother turned angrily.

"Now she's sold, and gone, and done with. So don't
ask any more questions. They won't change it. She's
gone, so that's that—and let's say no more about it."

"But Mother . . ."

The boy's cry rang out, high and puzzled. His
mother interrupted him.

"Now no more! Come and have your tea! Come on. Sit ye down!"

Obediently the boy went to his place at the table. The woman turned to the man at the fireplace.

"Come on, Sam, and eat. Though Lord knows, it's poor enough stuff to set out for tea . . ."

The woman grew quiet as her husband rose with an angry suddenness. Then, without speaking a word, he strode to the door, took his cap from a peg, and went out. The door slammed behind him. For a moment after, the cottage was silent. Then the woman's voice rose, scolding in tone.

"Now, see what ye've done! Got thy father all angry. I suppose ye're happy now."

Wearily she sat in her chair and stared at the table. For a long time the cottage was silent. Joe knew it was unfair of his mother to blame him for what was happening. Yet he knew, too, that it was his mother's way of covering up her own hurt. It was exactly the same as her scolding. That was the way with the people in those parts. They were rough, stubborn people, used to living a rough, hard life. When anything happened that touched their emotions, they covered up their feelings. The women scolded and chattered to hide their hurts. They did not mean anything by it. After it was over . . .

"Come on, Joe. Eat up!"

His mother's voice was soft and patient now.

The boy stared at his plate, unmoving.

"Come on, Joe. Eat your bread and butter. Look— nice new bread, I just baked today. Don't ye want it?"

The boy bent his head lower.

"I don't want any," he said in a whisper.

"Oh, dogs, dogs, dogs," his mother flared. Her voice rose in anger again. "All this trouble over one dog. Well, if ye ask me, I'm glad Lassie's gone. That I am.

As much trouble to take care of as a child! Now she's gone, and it's done with, and I'm glad—I am. I'm glad!"

Mrs. Carraclough shook her plump self and sniffed. Then she took her handkerchief from her apron pocket and blew her nose. Finally she looked at her son, still sitting, unmoving. She shook her head sadly and spoke. Again her voice was patient and kind.

"Joe, come here," she said.

The boy rose and stood by his mother. She put her plump arm around him and spoke, his head turned to the fire.

"Look Joe, ye're getting to be a big lad now, and ye can understand. Ye see—well, ye know things aren't going so well for us these days. Ye know how it is. And we've got to have food on the table, and we've got to pay our rent—and Lassie was worth a lot of money and—well, we couldn't afford to keep her, that's all. Now these are poor times and ye mustn't—ye mustn't upset thy father. He's worrying enough as it is—and—well, that's all. She's gone."

Young Joe Carraclough stood by his mother in the cottage. He did understand. Even a boy of twelve years in Greenall Bridge knew what "poor times" were.

For years, for as long as children could remember, their fathers had worked in the Wellington Pit beyond the village. They had gone on-shift, off-shift, carrying their snap boxes of food and their colliers' lanterns; and they had worked at bringing up the rich coal. Then times had become "poor." The pit went on "slack time," and the men earned less. Sometimes the work had picked up, and the men had gone on full time.

Then everyone was glad. It did not mean luxurious living for them, for in the coal-mining villages people lived a hard life at best. But it was a life of courage and family unity, at least, and if the food that was set on the tables was plain, there was enough of it to go round.

Only a few months ago, the pit had closed down altogether. The big wheel at the top of the shaft spun no more. The men no longer flowed in a stream to the pit-yard at the shift changes. Instead, they signed on at the Labor Exchange. They stood on the corner by the Exchange, waiting for work. But no work came. It seemed that they were in what the newspapers called "the stricken areas"—sections of the country from which all industry had gone. Whole villages of people were out of work. There was no way of earning a living. The Government gave the people a "dole"—a weekly sum of money—so that they could stay alive.

Joe knew this. He had heard people talking in the village. He had seen the men at the Labor Exchange. He knew that his father no longer went to work. He knew, too, that his father and mother never spoke of it before him—that in their rough, kind way they had tried to keep their burdens of living from bearing also on his young shoulders.

Though his brain told him these things, his heart still cried for Lassie. But he silenced it. He stood steadily and then asked one question.

"Couldn't we buy her back some day, Mother?"

"Now, Joe, she was a very valuable dog, and she's worth too much for us. But we'll get another dog some day. Just wait. Times might pick up, and then we'll get another pup. Wouldn't ye like that?"

Joe Carraclough bent his head and shook it slowly. His voice was only a whisper.

"I don't ever want another dog. Never! I only want—Lassie!"

An Evil-Tempered Old Man

The Duke of Rudling stood by a rhododendron hedge and glared about him. He lifted his voice again.

"Hynes!" he roared. "Hynes! Where has that chap got to? Hynes!"

At that moment, with his face red and his shock of white hair disordered, the Duke looked like what he was reputed to be: the worst-tempered old man in all the three Ridings of Yorkshire.

Whether or not he deserved this reputation, it would seem sufficient to say that his words and actions earned it.

Perhaps it was partly due to the fact that the Duke was exceedingly deaf, which caused him to speak to everyone as if he were commanding a brigade of infantry on parade, as indeed he had done, many years ago. He had also a habit of carrying a big blackthorn walking stick, which he always waved wildly in the air in order to give emphasis to his already too emphatic words. And finally, his bad temper came from his impatience with the world.

For the Duke had one firm belief: which was that the world was going, as he phrased it, "to pot." Nothing ever was as good these days as it had been when he was a young man. Horses could not run so fast, young men were not so brave and dashing, women were not so pretty, flowers did not grow so well, and as for dogs, if there were any decent ones left in the world, it was because they were in his own kennels.

The people could not even speak the King's English these days as they could when he was a young man, according to the Duke. He was firmly of the opinion that the reason he could not hear properly was not because he was deaf, but because people nowadays had got into the pernicious habit of mumbling and snipping their words instead of saying them plainly as they did when he was a young man.

And, as for the younger generation! The Duke could—and often would—lecture for hours on the worthlessness of everyone born in the twentieth century.

This last was curious, for of all his relatives, the only one the Duke could stand (and who could also stand the Duke, it seemed) was the youngest member of his family, his twelve-year-old granddaughter, Priscilla.

It was Priscilla who came to his rescue now as he stood, waving his stick and shouting, beside the rhododendron hedge.

Dodging a wild swish of his stick, she reached over and pulled the pocket of his tweed Norfolk coat. He turned with bristling moustaches.

"Oh, it's you!" he roared. "It's a wonder somebody finally came. Don't know what the world's coming to. Servants no good! Everybody too deaf to hear! Country's going to pot!"

"Nonsense," said Priscilla.

She was indeed a very self-contained and composed young lady. From her constant association with her grandfather, she had grown to consider them both as equals—either as old children or as very young grownups.

"What's that?" the Duke roared, looking down at her. "Speak up! Don't mumble!"

Priscilla pulled his head down so that she could speak directly into his ear.

"I said, *Nonsense!*" she shouted.

"Nonsense?" roared the Duke.

He stared down at her, then broke into a roar of laughter. He had a curious way of reasoning about Priscilla. He was convinced that if Priscilla had pluck enough to answer him back, she must have inherited it from him.

So the Duke felt in a much better temper as he looked down at his granddaughter. He flourished his long white moustaches, which were much grander and finer than the kind of moustaches that men manage to grow these days.

"Ah, glad you turned up," the Duke boomed. "I want you to see a new dog. She's marvelous! Beautiful! Finest collie I ever laid my eyes on."

"She isn't so good as the ones they had in the old days, is she?" Priscilla asked.

"Don't mumble," roared the Duke. "Can't hear a word you say."

He had heard perfectly well, but had decided to ignore it.

"Knew I'd get her," the Duke continued. "Been after her for three years now."

"Three years!" echoed Priscilla. She knew that was what her grandfather wanted her to say.

"Yes, three years. Ah, he thought he'd get the better of me, but he didn't. Offered him ten pound for her three years ago, but he wouldn't sell. Came up to twelve the year after that, but he wouldn't sell. Last year offered him fifteen pounds. Told him it was the limit—and I meant it, too. But he didn't think so. Held out for another six months, then he sent word last week he'd take it."

The Duke seemed pleased with himself, but Priscilla shook her head.

"How do you know she isn't coped?"

This was a natural question to ask, for if the truth must be told, Yorkshiremen are not only knowing about raising dogs, but they are sometimes alleged to carry their knowledge too far. Often they exercise devious secret arts in hiding faults in a dog: perhaps treating a crooked ear or a faulty tail carriage so that this drawback is absolutely imperceptible until much later, when the less-knowing purchaser has paid for the dog and has taken it home. These tricks and treatments are known as "coping." In the buying and selling of dogs—as with horses—the unwritten rule is *caveat emptor* (let the buyer beware!).

But the Duke only roared louder when he heard Priscilla's question.

"How do I know she isn't coped? Because I'm a Yorkshireman, too. Know as many tricks as they do, and a few more to boot, I'll warrant.

"No. This is a straight dog. Besides, I got her from Whatsisname—Carraclough. Know him too well. He wouldn't dare try anything like that on me. Indeed not!"

And the Duke swished his great blackthorn stick through the air as if to defy anyone who would have the courage to try any tricks on him. The old man and his grandchild went down the path to the kennels. And there, by the mesh-wire runs, they halted, looking at the dog inside.

Priscilla saw, lying there, a great black-white-and-golden-sable collie. It lay with its head across its front paws, the delicate darkness of the aristocratic head showing plainly against the snow-whiteness of the expansive ruff and apron.

The Duke clicked his tongue, in signal to the dog.

But she did not respond. There was only a flick of the ear to show that the dog had heard. She lay there, her eyes not turning toward the people who stood looking at her.

Priscilla bent down and, clapping her hands, called quickly:

"Come, collie! Come over here! Come see me! Come!"

For just one second the great brown eyes of the collie turned to the girl, deep brown eyes that seemed full of brooding and sadness. Then they turned back to mere empty staring.

Priscilla rose.

"She doesn't seem well, Grandfather!"

"Nonsense!" roared the Duke. "Nothing wrong with her. Hynes! Hynes! Where is that fellow hiding? Hynes!"

"Coming sir, coming!"

The sharp nasal voice of the kennelman came from behind the buildings, and in a moment he hurried into sight.

"Yes, sir! You called me, sir?"

"Of course, of course. Are you deaf? Hynes, what's the matter with this dog? She looks off-color."

"Well, sir, she's a poor feeder," the kennelman hurried to explain in a Cockney accent that made his "I's" sound like "Hi's." "She's spoiled, I should say. They spoils 'em in them cottages. Feeds 'em by and wiv a silver spoon, as ye might say. But I'll see she gets over it. She'll take her food kennel way in a few days, sir."

"Well, keep an eye on her, Hynes!" the Duke shouted. "You keep a good eye on that dog!"

"Yes, sir. I will, sir," Hynes answered dutifully.

"You'd better, too," the Duke said.

Then he went muttering away. Somehow he was disappointed. He had wanted Priscilla to see the fine new purchase he had made. Instead, she had seen a scornful dog.

He heard her speaking.

"What did you say?"

She lifted her head.

"I said, why did the man sell you his dog?"

The Duke stood a moment, scratching behind his ear.

"Well, he knew I'd reached my limit, I suppose. Told him I wouldn't give him a penny more, and I suppose he finally came to the conclusion that I meant it. That's all."

As they went together back toward the great old house, Hynes, the kennelman, turned to the dog in the run.

"I'll see ye eat before I'm through," he said. "I'll see ye eat if I 'ave to push it down yer throat."

The dog gave no motion in answer. She only blinked her eyes as if ignoring the man on the other side of the wire.

When he was gone, she lay unmoving in the sunshine, until the shadows became longer. Then, uneasily she rose. She lifted her head to scent the breeze. As if she had not read there what she desired, she whimpered lightly. She began patrolling the wire, going back and forth—back and forth.

She was a dog, and she could not think in terms of thoughts such as we may put in words. There was only in her mind and in her body a growing desire that was at first vague. But then the desire became plainer and plainer. The time sense in her drove at her brain and muscles.

Suddenly, Lassie knew what it was she wanted. Now she knew.

Lassie Comes Home Again

When Joe Carraclough came out of school and walked through the gate, he could not believe his eyes. He stood for a moment, and then his voice rang shrill. "Lassie! Lassie!"

He ran to his dog, and in his moment of wild joy he knelt beside her, plunging his fingers deep into her rich coat. He buried his face in her mane and patted her sides.

He stood again and almost danced with excitement. There was strange contrast between the boy and the dog. The boy was lifted above himself with gladness, but the dog sat calmly, only by the wave of her white-tipped tail saying she was glad to see him.

It was as if she said: "What's there to be excited about? I'm supposed to be here, and here I am. What's so wonderful in all that?"

"Come, Lassie," the boy said.

He turned and ran down the street. For a second he did not reason out the cause of her being there. When the wonder of it struck him, he pushed it away.

Why question how this wonderful thing had happened? It was enough that it had happened.

But his mind would not stay at rest. He quieted it again.

Had Father bought the dog back again? Perhaps that was it!

He raced on down High Street, and now Lassie seemed to catch his enthusiasm. She ran beside him, leaping high in the air, barking that sharp cry of happiness that dogs often can achieve. She stretched her mouth wide, as collies so frequently do in their glad moments and in a way that makes collie owners swear that their dogs laugh when pleased.

It was not until he was passing the Labor Exchange that Joe slowed down. Then he heard the voice of one of the men calling: "Eigh, lad. Wheer'd tha find thy dog again?"

The tones were spoken in the broadest Yorkshire accent, and it was in the same accent that Joe answered. For, while in school all the children spoke "pure" English, it was considered polite to answer adults in the same accents they used.

"She were bi' t' school gate," Joe shouted.

But after that he knew the truth. His father had not bought the dog back again, or else all the men would have known it. In a small village like Greenall Bridge, everyone knew the business of everyone else. And certainly, in that particular village, they would have known about any such important matter as the resale of Lassie.

Lassie had escaped! That was it!

And so young Joe Carraclough ran gladly no more. He walked slowly, wonderingly, as he turned up the hillside lane to his home. By his door he turned and spoke to the dog sadly. "Stay at heel, Lassie," he said.

With his brow furrowed in thought, he stood outside the door. He made his face appear blank of expression. He opened the door and walked in.

"Mother," he said. "I've got a surprise."

He held out his hand toward her, as if this gesture would help him get what he most desired.

"Lassie's come home," he said.

He saw his mother staring at him. His father looked up from his place by the fire. Then, as Joe came into the cottage, he saw their eyes turn to the dog that followed obediently at his heel. They stared, but they did not speak.

As if the collie understood this silence, she paused a moment. Then she walked, going head down as a dog will when it feels that it has done something—it does not know what—that is wrong. She went to the hearth rug and wagged her tail as if in signal that no matter what sins had been committed, she was willing to make up again.

But there seemed to be no forgiveness, for the man turned his eyes from her suddenly and stared into the fire. That way the man shut his dog from his sight.

The dog slowly coiled herself and sank to the rug, so that her body touched the man's foot. He drew it away. The dog lay her head across her paw and then, like the man, stared into the depths of the fire, as if in that golden fancyland there would be an answer to all their troubles.

It was the woman who moved first. She put her hands on her hips and sighed a long, audible sigh—one that was eloquent of exasperation. Joe looked at her and then, to try to soften their stoniness, he began speaking, his voice bright with hope.

"I was coming out of school, and there she was. Right where she always is. Right at the gate waiting for me. And you never saw anyone as glad to see you. She wagged her tail at me. She was that glad to see me."

Joe spoke on, the words racing from him. It was as if as long as he could keep on talking, neither his mother nor his father could say the dread words that he expected to hear. With his flood of speech, he would hold back the sentence.

"I could see she was that homesick for us—for all of

us. So I thought I'd bring her right along, and we could just . . ."

"No!"

It was his mother, interrupting loudly. It was the first word that either of the parents had spoken. For a second Joe stood still, and then the words flooded from him again, making a fight for what he wanted and what he dared not hope he could have.

"But she's come home, Mother. We could hide her. They wouldn't know. We could say we hadn't seen her and then they'd . . ."

"No!" His mother's voice repeated the word sternly.

She turned away angrily and continued to set the table. Again she found relief, as the village women did, in scolding. Her voice ran on, with the words coming cold and sharp, to cover up her own feelings.

"Dogs, dogs, dogs!" she cried. "I'm fair sick o' hearin' about them. I won't have it. She's sold and gone and done with, and the sooner she's out o' my sight the better I'll be pleased. Now get her out o' here. And hurry up, or first thing you know we'll have that Hynes comin' 'round here. That Mr. Know-It-All Hynes!"

Her voice sharpened with the last words, for she pronounced them in imitation of Hynes's way of speaking. The Duke of Rudling's kennelman was from London, and his clipped Cockney accent always seemed to irritate the local people, whose speech was broad-vowelled and slow.

"Now, that's my say," Joe's mother went on. "So you might just as well put it in your pipe and smoke it. She's sold, so take her right back to them that's bought her."

Feeling there was no help coming from his mother, Joe turned to his father sitting before the fire. But his father sat as if he had not heard a word spoken. Joe's underlip crept out stubbornly, as he sought for some new means of argument. But it was Lassie who argued for herself. Now that the cottage was silent she seemed to think all trouble was passed. Slowly she rose and, going to the man, began nudging his hand with her slim muzzle, as a dog so often will when it wants attention and comfort from its master. But the man drew his hand away from the dog's reach and went on staring into the fire.

Joe watched that. He turned a soft argument on his father. "Eigh, Father," he said, sadly. "Ye might at least bid her welcome. It isn't her fault, and she's that glad to be home. Just pat her."

Joe's father gave no sign that he had heard his son's words.

"Ye know, happen they don't care for her right up at the kennels," Joe went on, as if speaking to the open air of the cottage. "D'ye think they understand how to feed her properly?

"Now, for instance, look at her coat. It does look a bit poorly, doesn't it? Father, don't ye think just a bit o' linseed strained through her drinking water would bring it up a little? That's what I'd do for a dog that could stand a bit brighter coat, wouldn't ye, Father?"

Still looking in the fire, Joe's father began nodding slowly. But if he did not seem aware of his son's attack, Mrs. Carraclough understood it. She sniffed.

"Aye," she stormed at her son. "Tha wouldn't be a Carraclough—nor a Yorkshireman—if tha didn't know more about tykes than breaking eggs with a stick."

Her voice droned on in the cottage.

"My goodness, sometimes it seems to me that the men in this village think more o' their tykes than they do o' their flesh and blood. That they do. Here's hard times, and do they get work? No. They go on the dole, and I swear some will be quite content to let their own children go hungry as long as the dog gets fed."

Joe's father shifted his feet uneasily, but the boy interrupted quickly.

"But truly, Mother, she does look thin. I'll bet you anything they're not feeding her right."

"Well," she answered pertly, "at that I wouldn't put it past Mister Know-It-All Hynes to steal best part of the dog meat for himself. For I never saw a skinnier-looking, meaner-faced man in all my life."

During this flow of words her eyes had turned to the dog. And suddenly her tone changed. "By gum," she said. "She does look a bit poorly. Poor thing, I'd better fix her a little something. She can do with it, or I don't know dogs."

Then Mrs. Carraclough seemed to realize that her sympathies were directly opposed to the words she had been speaking five minutes before. As if to defend herself and excuse herself, she lifted her voice:

"But the minute she's fed, back she goes," she scolded. "And when she's gone, never another tyke will I have in my house. All ye do is bring 'em up and work over 'em—and they're as much trouble as raisin' a child. And after all your work's done, what do you get for it?"

Thus, chattering angrily, Mrs. Carraclough warmed a pan of food. She set it before the dog, and she and her son stood watching Lassie eat happily. But the man never once turned his eyes toward the dog that had been his.

When Lassie had finished eating, Mrs. Carraclough picked up the plate. Joe went to the mantlepiece and took down a folded piece of cloth and a brush. He sat on the hearth rug and began prettying the dog's coat.

At first, the man kept his eyes on the fire. Then, despite his efforts, he began to turn quick glances toward the boy and the dog beside him. At last, as if he could stand it no longer, he turned and held out his hand.

"That's no way to do it, lad," he said, with his rough voice full of warmth. "If ye're off to do a job, ye might as well learn to do it right. See thee—like this!"

He took the brush and cloth from his son and, kneeling on the rug, began working expertly on the dog's coat, rubbing the rich, deep coat with the cloth, cradling the aristocratic muzzle carefully in one hand, while with the other he worked over the snow white of the collie's ruff and artistically fluffed out the "leggings" and the "apron" and the "petticoats."

So for a spell, there was quiet happiness in the cottage. The man lost all other thought as he gave his mind over to the work. Joe sat on the rug beside him, watching each turn of the brush and remembering it; for he knew—as in fact every man in the village knew—that there was not a man for miles around who could groom a collie either for work-day or for show bench as could Sam Carraclough, his father. And his greatest dream and ambition was to be, some day, as fine a dog-man as his father.

It was Mrs. Carraclough who seemed to remember first what they had all driven from their minds, that Lassie no longer belonged to them.

"Now please," she cried, in exasperation. "Will ye get that tyke out o' here?"

Joe's father turned in sudden anger. His voice was thick with the Yorkshire accent that deepened the speech of all the men of the village.

"Ye wouldn't have me taking her back lewking like a mucky Monday wash, would'ta?"

"Look, Sam, please," the woman began. "If ye don't hurry her back . . ."

She paused, and they all listened. There was the sound of footsteps coming up the garden path.

"There," she cried, in exasperation. "It's that Hynes!"

She ran toward the door, but before she reached it, it opened, and Hynes came in. The small, thin figure in its checked coat, riding breeches, and cloth leggings halted for a moment. Then Hynes's eye turned to the dog before the hearth.

"Ow, I thought so," he cried. "I just thought as 'ow I'd find 'er 'ere."

Joe's father rose slowly.

"I were just cleaning her up a bit," he said ponderously, "and then I were off to bring her back."

"I'll bet ye were," Hynes mocked. "Ye were going to bring 'er back—I'll bet ye were. But it just so 'appens that I'll take 'er back myself—since I 'appened to drop in."

Taking a leash from his pocket, he walked quickly to the collie and slipped the noose over her head. At the tug she rose obediently and, with her tail down, followed the man to the door. There Hynes halted.

"Ye see," he said, in parting. "I wasn't born yesterday, and I 'appen to know a trick or two myself. You Yorkshiremen! I know all about ye and yer come-home dogs. Training 'em to break loose and run right back 'ome when they're sold, so then ye can sell 'em to someone else. Well, it won't work with me, it won't. Because I know a trick or two myself, I do . . ."

He halted suddenly, for Joe's father, his face deep red with anger, had started toward the door.

"Er—Good evening," Hynes said quickly.

Then the door closed, and Hynes and the collie were gone. For a long time there was silence in the cottage, and then Mrs. Carraclough's voice rose.

"I won't have it, I won't," she cried, "Walkin' into my house and home without so much as by your leave, and keeping his hat on as if he thinks he's the very

Duke himself. And all on account of a dog. Well, she's
gone, and if you ask me, I say good riddance. Now
happen we can have a little peace. I hope I never see
her again, I do."

As she scolded, her tongue running on, Joe and his
father sat before the fire. Now both of them stared into
it, unmoving and patient, each burying his own
thoughts inside himself as the north-country people do
when they are deeply troubled.

"Don't Come Home Any More"

If Mrs. Carraclough thought that everything was set-tled, she was mistaken, for the next day Lassie was at the school gate, keeping her faithful tryst, waiting for Joe.

And again Joe brought her home. On his way, he planned to fight for his dog. To him the course was simple. He felt that when his parents saw the dog's faithfulness, they would relent and let her stay with them again, and thus reward her. But he knew it would not be easy for him to persuade them.

Slowly he walked up the path with the dog and opened the door. Everything in the cottage was as it had been before—his mother getting the evening meal ready, his father brooding in front of the fire as he did for hours these days since there was no work.

"She's—she's come home again," Joe said.

All his hopes fled at his mother's first words. There was no surrender in them.

"I won't have it. No, I won't have it," she cried. "Ye can't bring her in—and it's no use begging and plagu-ing me. She's got to go right back! Right this minute!"

The words cascaded over Joe. In the strict bringing-up of his Yorkshire home, with its stern kindness, it was rare that he "answered back," as the saying is, to his parents. But this time he felt he must try, must make them understand.

"But Mother, just a little while. Please, just a little while. Let me keep her just a little while!"

He felt that if he could only keep her there a short time, the hearts of his parents would soften. Perhaps Lassie felt that, too, for as Joe talked she walked in and went to her accustomed place on the hearth rug. As if she knew the talk was of her, she lay down, turning her eyes from one to another of the humans who usually spoke so quietly, but whose voices now were harsh.

"It's no use, Joe. The longer ye keep her here, the harder it's going to be to take her back. And go back she must!"

"But Mother—Father, look, please. She doesn't look well. They don't feed her right. Don't you think . . ."

Joe's father got up and faced his son. The man's face was blank and emotionless, but his voice was full of understanding.

"That won't work this time, Joe," he said, ponderously. "Ye see, lad, it's no use. We must take her back right after tea."

"No! Ye'll take her back this very minute," Mrs. Carraclough cried. "If ye don't, ye'll have that Hynes round here again. And I won't have him walking into my house as if he owned it. Now put on your cap and go this very minute."

"She'll only come back again, Mother. Don't you see, she'll only come back again. She's our dog . . ."

Joe stopped as his mother sank down in a chair in a movement of weariness. She looked at her husband, and he nodded, as if to say Joe was right.

"She comes back for the lad, ye see," the father said.

"I can't help it, Sam. She's got to go," Mrs. Carraclough said slowly. "And if it's the lad she comes back for, then ye must take him with ye. Let him go with ye, and he must put her in the kennels and tell her to stay. If he bid her rest there, happen she'd understand and be content, and not run away home any more."

"Aye, there's sense to that," the man said, slowly. "Get thy cap, Joe, and come wi' me."

Miserably Joe got his cap. The man made a soft whistling sound. Lassie rose obediently. Then the man, the boy, and the dog left the cottage. Behind him, Joe could hear his mother's voice still going on, but full of weariness, as if she would soon cry from her tiredness.

"If she'd stay at the kennel, then happen we could have a little peace and quiet in the home, though heaven knows there's not much chance of that these days, things being what they are . . ."

Joe heard her voice trail away as, silently, he followed his father and Lassie.

"Grandfather," Priscilla said, "can animals hear things that we can't?"

"Oh, yes. Yes. Of course," the Duke roared. "Take a dog, now. Hears five times as well as a human being. For instance, my silent dog whistle. It isn't silent, really. Makes high frequency sounds, but we don't hear them. No human can. Dog hears them, though, and comes running. That's because . . ."

Priscilla saw her grandfather start and then begin waving his blackthorn stick menacingly as he went down the path.

"Carraclough! What're ye doing there with my dog?"

Priscilla saw down the path a great, tall, village man and beside him a sturdy boy, who stood with his hand resting lightly on the mane of a collie. She heard the dog growl softly, as if in protest at the menacing advance of her grandfather, and then—the low voice of the boy quieting the dog. She followed her grandfather toward the strangers.

Sam Carraclough, seeing her coming, lifted his cap and poked his son to do likewise. This was not in any sense a servile gesture, but because many of the rough village people prided themselves in being well brought-up and conducting themselves with politeness.

"It's Lassie," Carraclough said.

"Of course it's Lassie," the Duke boomed. "Any fool can see that. What're ye doing with her?"

"She's run away again, and I'm bringing her back to you."

"Again? Has she run away before?"

Sam Carraclough stood silent. Like most of the village people, his mind moved very slowly. From the Duke's last words, he realized that Hynes had not told of her previous escape. And if he answered the Duke's question, he felt that in some way he would be telling tales on Hynes. Even though he disliked Hynes, he could not tell on him, for, as he phrased it in his own honest mind, he "wouldn't like to do a man out of his job." Hynes might be discharged, and jobs were hard to get these days. Sam Carraclough knew that.

He solved his problem in a typical Yorkshire way. Stubbornly he repeated his last words.

"I'm bringing her back—that's all."

The Duke stared at him menacingly. Then he lifted his voice even louder.

"Hynes! Hynes! Why does that man always run away and hide every time I want him? Hynes!"

"Coming, sir. Coming," came the nasal voice.

Soon Hynes came hustling from behind the shrubberies beside the kennels.

"Hynes, has this dog broken away before?"

Hynes squirmed uneasily.

"Well, sir, it's this way . . ."

"Did she or didn't she?"

"In a way, sir, she did——but I didn't want to disturb Your Grace abour 'er," Hynes said, fingering his cap nervously. "But I'll jolly well see she doesn't get away again. Can't think 'ow she did it. I wired up all the places she dug underneath, and I'll see . . ."

"You'd better!" the Duke shouted. "Utter nincompoop! That's what! I begin to think you're an utter nincompoop, Hynes! Pen her up. And if she breaks out again, I'll——I'll . . ."

The Duke did not finish explaining what dire things he intended to do, but instead went stumping away in an evil temper without so much as a "thank you" to Sam Carraclough.

Priscilla somehow felt that, for she started to follow her grandfather but then halted. She turned and, standing quietly, watched the scene he had left. Hynes was stirring angrily.

"I'll pen 'er up," he muttered. "And if she ever gets away again, I'll . . ."

He did not finish the sentence, for as he spoke he made as if to grasp Lassie's mane. But he never reached the dog, for Sam Carraclough's heavy, hobnailed boot trod on Hynes's foot, pinning him to his position. The man spoke slowly.

"I brought my lad wi' me to pen her up this time," he said. "It's him she runs for, and so he'll pen her up and bid her stay."

Then the cumbrous Yorkshire voice lifted, as if Sam Carraclough had just noticed something.

"Eigh, now I'm sorry. I didn't hardly notice I were standing on thy foot. Come along, Joe, lad. Unlatch the kennel for us, Hynes, and we'll put her in."

Priscilla, standing still beside the aged evergreens,

saw the dog come through from the kennel to the run.
As the boy came by the wire, the collie lifted her head,
then walked to him, and pressed against the wire. For a
long moment the boy stood there, his fingers reaching
through the mesh to touch the coolness of the dog's
nose. The man ended the silence.

"Come on, Joe, lad. Now get it over with. There's
no use stretching it out. Bid her stay—tell her we can't
have her coming home no more."

Priscilla saw the boy by the kennels look up at his
father and then glance around, as if there would be
some help coming from somewhere.

But there was none. There was no help anywhere
for Joe. He swallowed and started to speak, his words
coming slowly, in a low tone, but getting faster and
faster as he spoke.

"Stay here and bide happy, Lassie," he began, his
voice hardly audible. "And—and don't come home no
more. Don't run away no more. Don't come to school
for me no more. Stay here and let us be—because—ye
don't belong to us no more, and we don't want to see
thee—ever, again. Because tha's a bad dog—and we
don't love thee no more, and we don't want to see thee.
So don't plague us and come running home—and stay
here forever and leave us be. And—and don't never
come home again!"

The dog, as if she understood, walked to the far corner of the kennel and lay down. The boy turned savagely and started away. And because it was hard for
him to see where he was going, he stumbled. But his
father, who was walking beside him with his head very
high and his gaze straight ahead, caught him by the
shoulder and shook him and said roughly:

"Look where tha's going!"

Joe trotted beside his father, who walked quickly.

He was thinking that he would never be able to understand why grownups were so hard-hearted just when you needed them most.

He ran beside his father, thinking that, and not understanding that the man wanted to get away from the sound that followed them—the sound of a collie, barking bravely, calling to her master not to desert her. Joe did not understand that.

And there was another who found many things hard to understand. It was Priscilla, who came closer to the run where the collie now stood, her eyes fixed unmovingly on the spot where she had last seen her master turn the corner down the path, her head lifting with the signal bark.

Priscilla watched the dog until Hynes came from the front of the kennels. She called to him.

"Hynes!"

"Why does the dog run home to them? Isn't she happy here?"

"Why, bless yer 'eart, Miss Priscilla, of course she's 'appy—a fine kennel like she's got. She just runs 'ome because they've trained 'er to do it. That's the way they do—steal 'em back and sell 'em to somebody else before ye could say Bob's-yer-uncle."

Priscilla wrinkled her nose in thought.

"But if they wanted to steal her back, why did they return her themselves?"

"Now just ye don't worry yer pretty 'ead about it," Hynes said. "It's just ye can't trust none o' them down in that village. They're always up to tricks, they are— but we're too smart for 'em."

Priscilla thought a while.

"But if the boy wanted his dog back, why did they ever sell her in the first place? If she was my dog, I wouldn't sell her."

"Of course ye wouldn't, Miss Priscilla."

"Then why did they?"

"Why did they? Because yer grandfather paid 'em a bloomin' good price for 'er, 'e did. That's why. A bloomin' good price. 'E's too easy on 'em, that's what. If I 'ad my way—I'd make 'em step a bit. That I would, indeed!"

Satisfied with his solution, Hynes turned to the dog, which still stood barking its signal.

"Quiet, now. Go on. Down wiv yer! In yer kennel and lie down. Go on!"

As the dog made no sign of having heard him, Hynes strode nearer and lifted his hand in a striking gesture.

Slowly Lassie turned, and from her chest sounded a bass rumbling, and the lips crept upward so that the great teeth shone whitely. Her ears drew back, and the mane on her neck rose slowly. The rumbling growl sounded louder.

Hynes halted, and he rolled his tongue between his gaping front teeth.

"Oh, so ye'd get nasty, would yer?" he said.

Then Priscilla walked before him.

"Look out, Miss Priscilla. I wouldn't go too near if I were you. She'd just as leaf take a bite out o' yer as look at yer, if I knows dogs. Which I do! But I'll 'ave the fine lady stepping around afore I'm through with 'er, that I will. So you keep away from 'er, Miss."

And Hynes turned away. For a long time Priscilla stood. Then slowly she walked to the wiring. She put her fingers through so that they were close to Lassie's head.

"Come here, then, girl," she said, softly. "Come to me. Come on! I wouldn't hurt you. Come on!"

The dog's growling subsided, and she sank to the ground. For one second her great brown eyes met the blue ones of the girl. Then the dog ignored her and,

with a sort of suffering aristrocratic majesty, lay in the
pen. Her eyes did not blink, and her head did not turn.
She lay there, staring steadily at the spot where she had
last seen Sam Carraclough and his son.

The Hiding Place on the Moor

The next day Lassie lay in her pen, the early summer sunlight streaming over her coat. Her head rested on her paws. It was pointing in the direction that Sam Carraclough and his son had gone the evening before. Her eyes were lifted, thrown forward, so that, although her body was at rest, her senses were awake to any sight or sound or smell that might mean her masters were returning.

But the afternoon was quiet. There was a hum of early bees in the air, the smell of the damp English countryside. That was all.

The afternoon deepened, and Lassie began to stir. There was some impulse warning her faintly. It was indistinct, indefinable, perhaps as when an alarm clock rings to disturb, but dimly, a still-sleeping human being.

Lassie lifted her head suddenly and scented the breeze. But this did not give her any quieting answer to the vague stirrings within her.

She got up, walked slowly toward the kennel, and lay down in the shade. That did not bring her any ease. She got up again and went back to the sun; but that was not the answer. The curious urging in her mind drove more strongly. She began walking about the pen, circling, pacing by the stout mesh-wire. The force within her drove her to walking round and round mak-

ing circle after circle about her cage. Then in one corner she halted, and with her paw she clawed the wire.

As if that were the signal, she suddenly understood
her desire. It was time! Time to go for the boy! Not
that she thought this plainly, as a human being might,
she knew it only blindly. But the impulse held her en-
tirely and drove everything else away from her feeling
or awareness. She only knew that it was time to go to
the school, as she had gone every day for so many
years.

Although she clawed vigorously at the wire, she
made little impression. Memory told her she had escaped there before, clawing, tearing at the wire, then
digging and squeezing underneath, lifting with her
powerful neck and back muscles so that she could be
free. But Hynes had cut off that path to escape. He had
reinforced the mesh of the pen with even stouter wire,
and had driven stout stakes of wood into the ground
beside it. No matter how Lassie clawed and fought it
was no use. As if her defeat and the passing of time
forced her to even more energy, Lassie raced about inside the pen. She scratched at places where her instinct
told her there might be a path to safety, but Hynes had
reinforced them all.

Frantically she lifted her head to bark in frustrated
anger, and then, tentatively, she reared and stood on
her hind legs against the wire, looking up.

If you could go under a thing, you might go over it!

Dogs can know these things not by logical thought
processes, or because someone has told them it must be
so. Even the very smartest dogs learn them only
slowly, led by hazy instinct and by the training they
have had in their own short lives.

So, dimly, and then more clearly, the new idea came
into Lassie's mind. She leaped, and fell back again.

The fence was six feet high, much too high for a collie to leap. A greyhound or borzoi could have sailed over it easily. Dogs have been bred throughout the years to develop types to meet varying needs. Collies are of that group called working dogs, raised for centuries to work with man, to understand his words and signs, to be intelligent and helpful, especially in shepherding. In these things they excel; but they cannot leap or race as can other types of dogs that have been perfected for those qualities alone.

Lassie's leaping, therefore, brought her nowhere near the top of the wire. She turned back the length of her pen and raced in a running start, but each time she fell back.

It seemed impossible, but with the courage and persistence of a good animal, she tried again and again, leaping at different spots, as if one place might be more accessible than another.

And one place was!

She jumped right at the corner, where the mesh joined at a right angle, and, while she was in the air, her driving hind legs found some support in the angle of the fence.

She tried again and this time, almost like a man climbing a ladder, she scrambled higher in a wild flurry of energy. She was almost at the top, and then she fell back.

But she had learned quickly. She turned and ran again, this time held against the angle of wire by her own driving rush. Her feet clawed at the wire in that instant when the force of gravity was overcome. She struggled higher and higher, and her front paws reached the top. For a single second she hung there. And then slowly she pulled herself upward. She teetered a moment, uncertainly. The top of the wire clawed at her belly. But she did not feel it. Only one thought was in her mind. It was time, the time to keep faith at a meeting place.

She launched herself out and dropped to the ground outside the pen. She was free!

Now that she had achieved it, it seemed that all angry energy had left her. She had a clear way, yet instinct drove her to a new action. As if she knew that she would be captured again if she were seen, she moved warily as a dog can when it is hunting or being hunted.

With her belly close to the ground, she slid across the path silently to the rhododendron thicket. The heavy foliage swallowed her. A second later she was gliding like a ghost in the shadow of a wall far away. Her memory of terrain, like that of most animals, was perfect. She went silently, but with amazing speed, to a spot where the wall ended and the iron-paling fence began. There was a hole under the fence there that she had found before. She slid through it.

As if she understood that this was the limit of a sort of enemy territory, her way of going was not changed. She became normal again. She trotted calmly, her head erect, her full tail flowing behind in a graceful continuation of the curving lines of her body. She was just a glorious collie, trotting along happily, going through a routine of life without fuss or excitement.

Joe Carraclough had never expected to see Lassie any more. After he had bidden her stay, after he had scolded her for running home, he had really believed that she would never come to meet him any more at school.

But somewhere, down far in the depths of his hopes, he had dreamed of it, without ever believing his dream would come true. And when he came from school that

day and saw Lassie waiting, exactly as usual, he felt
that it was not true—he was only living in his dreams.

He stared at his dog, his broad, boyish face full of
amazement. Then, as if his silence were a sign that her
behavior had been worthy of disapproval, Lassie
dropped her head. She wagged her tail slowly, asking
forgiveness for the unknown sin she had committed.

Joe Carraclough dropped his hand to touch her
neck.

"It's all right, Lassie," he said slowly. "It's all right."

He did not look at the dog. For his mind was racing,
going far, far away in thought. He was remembering
how, twice before, he had brought his dog home. And
yet, despite all his hopes and pleadings, she had been
taken away.

So he did not hurry gladly toward his home this
time. Instead, he stood, his hand resting on the neck of
his dog, his forehead wrinkling as he tried to puzzle out
this problem of his life.

Hynes thundered at the cottage door and walked in
without waiting for an answer.

"Come on, where is she?" he demanded.

Mr. and Mrs. Carraclough stared at him, and then
their glances turned toward each other. The woman,
with troubled eyes, seemed to pay no attention to
Hynes.

"So that's why he's not home!" she said.

"Aye," the man agreed.

"They're together—him and Lassie. She's got away
again, and he's afraid to come home. He knows we'll
take her back. He's run away with her so's we can't
take her back."

She dropped into a chair, and her voice became un-
steady.

"Oh, my heavens! Shall I *never* have any peace and

quiet in my home? Never any peace any more?"

Her husband rose slowly. Then he went to the door.
He took his cap from the peg and went back to his
wife.

"Now don't thee worry, lass," he said. "Joe'll not
have gone far, just up on the moors he'll head. And he
won't get lost—both him and Lassie knows the moors
too well for that."

Hynes seemed to ignore the despair of the people in
the cottage. "Now, come on," he said. "Where's that
there dog o' mine?"

Slowly Sam Carraclough turned to the little man.

"That's what I'm off to find out, isn't it?" he said
mildly.

"Well, I'll just go along wiv, yer," Hynes said. "Just
to make sure there ain't no monkey business."

For a moment, a great anger surged in Sam Carraclough, and he strode toward the other man. Hynes
quailed quickly.

"Now don't ye start no trouble," he piped. "Ye'd
better not start no trouble."

Carraclough stared down at the smaller man, and
then, as if scorning one so beneath him in size and
spirit, he went to the door. There he turned.

"Ye'll just go right home, Mr. Hynes," he said. "Thy
dog'll be back to thee, just as soon as I find her."

Then Sam Carraclough went out into the dark evening. He did not go to the village. Instead he went up
the hill on the side lane, until he had reached the great,
flat table-land that stretched, foreboding and bleak, for
mile after mile over the Northern country.

He tramped forward steadily. It was soon dark, but
as if by instinct his feet kept to the lightly worn paths
that men had made in the hundreds of years of their
going and coming over the wild country. A stranger
might soon be lost in that land where there seemed no

landmarks for guidance, but not any of the village men.

All their lives—when children at play—they had learned their country. They knew every inch of the moorland, and a twist in a path spoke to them as surely of their whereabouts as a street sign on a corner does to a city dweller.

Surely then, Joe's father strode, for he knew where to look for his son. Five miles over the moor the land broke into what was an island in the flatness, an island of outcropping rocks, great sharp-edged blocks that looked much as if in some strange long ago a giant child had begun to pile up building-block towers and then had deserted the game while it was only half finished. It was there that the village people often wandered in their hours of trouble. The gaunt, forbidding rock towers, with their passages and caves, formed a place where one could sit in the vast silence and puzzle upon the problems of the world and of life without being disturbed by anyone.

And it was there that Sam Carraclough strode. He walked steadily through the darkness. The night rain began sweeping over the moor, fine and mist-like and insistent, but he did not slacken his step. At last the stone pile half loomed in the dark. And then, as his feet stepped on the first echoing stones, Sam Carraclough heard a sharp bark—the bark of a dog on watch, sounding a warning.

Climbing up on a path he remembered well from his own childhood, the man went toward the sound. And there, in the lee of a rock that sheltered them from the drive of the rain, he found the dog and his son. For a moment he stood, and there was only the sound of his breathing. Then the man said:

"Come, Joe."

That was all.

Obediently the boy rose, and in miserable silence he

followed his father. Together with the dog they went along the paths over the tangled heath grass, the paths they both knew so well. When they were near the village again, his father spoke once more.

"Go right home and wait up for me, Joe. I'm taking her back to the kennels. Then, when I get home, I want a word with thee."

What that "word" would be, Joe knew well. He knew he had offended the life of the family by running away. And how deeply that offense had cut his parents, he fully realized by the actions of his mother when he reached the cottage. She did not speak as he took off his soaking coat and set his shoes to dry by the hearth. She set food before him, a bowl of steaming tea. But still she did not speak.

Then, at last, his father was back again, standing in the cottage, his stern face glistening with the dampness of rain, and the light of the lamp cutting sharp reflections over his nose and cheekbones and chin.

"Joe," the man began. "Tha knows that tha's done wrong by running away wi' Lassie—done wrong to thy mother and to me?"

Joe looked steadily at his father. He lifted his head and spoke clearly. "Aye, Father."

His father nodded and took a deep breath. Then he put his hands to his waist and unbuckled his thick leather belt.

Joe watched silently. Then, to his surprise, he heard his mother speaking.

"Ye'll not," she cried. "I say ye'll not."

She was standing now, facing his father. Joe had never seen his mother quite like that before. She was standing there, face to face with his father. She turned quickly.

"Joe, go right upstairs to bed. Off ye go."

As Joe went obediently, he saw her turn back to his father and speak clearly.

"There's things to talk of first," she was saying. "And I'm off to speak 'em right here and now. I think it's time someone did."

The two were silent, and then as Joe passed his mother on the way to the stairs, she took him by the shoulders and for a second smiled into his face. She pressed his head quickly against her and then, with a kind of motion of her hand, pushed him toward the steps.

As Joe went upstairs he was wondering why it was that grownups sometimes were so understanding, just when you needed them most.

The next morning at breakfast nothing was said of the matter while his father was there.

Joe remembered that after he had gone upstairs the night before, long after he was in bed, his father and mother had talked. Once he had wakened to hear them still talking below. In the stoutly built cottage he had not heard the words—only the sounds of the voices: his mother's urgent and persistent, and his father's, low and rumbling and patient.

But when his father had finished breakfast and had gone out, Joe's mother began:

"Joe, I promised thy father I'd talk to thee."

Joe bent his gaze to the table and waited.

"Now tha knows tha did wrong, lad, doesn'ta?"

"Aye, Mother. I'm sorry."

"I know, but being sorry afterwards doesn't help at the time, Joe. And it's very important, for tha mustn't worry thy father. Not at this time, tha mustn't."

She sat, plump and motherly, at the table, looking

into Joe's face. Then her gaze seemed to go beyond him.

"Ye see, things ain't like what they used to be, Joe. And ye must remember that. Thy father, well, he's got a lot on his mind these days with things as they are. Tha's a big lad now, tha's twelve years old—and tha's got to try to understand things as if tha's more grown up.

"Now, it's hard just now making things go right in a home. And it does take a lot to feed a tyke, to feed it properly, that is. She had a very good appetite, Lassie did, and it's hard work to feed 'em properly these days, things being as they are. Now do ye understand?"

Joe nodded slowly. In a way he half understood. If grownups could only see it the way he did, he wanted to say that. But his mother was patting his arm, patting it with the hand that was so clean and shiny and plump, the hand that kneaded the bread and moved so quickly when there were stockings to knit, and that danced over the needle when there was darning.

"That's a good lad, Joe."

Her face brightened."

"And happen some day, things'll all be changed again—and it'll be like old times again—and then, first thing ye know, we'll get another dog, shall we?"

Joe did not know why, but it seemed as though the oatmeal were stuck in his throat.

"But I don't want another dog," he cried. "Not ever. I don't want another dog."

He wanted to say, too, "I only want Lassie."

But he knew somehow that this would hurt his mother. So instead he took his cap and ran from the house, down the lane to where the others were going to school.

Nothing Left but Honesty

It was just as his mother had said. Things were not as they used to be. Joe felt that more and more as the days passed. For one thing, Lassie came no more to the school. It seemed that at last the Duke's kennelman must have invented some manner of surrounding her with obstacles that even she could not surmount.

Each day when Joe came out of school, hope would run high for a moment, and he would turn his eyes to the place by the gate where she had always sat. But she was never there.

During the hours in school, Joe would try to think of his lessons, but his mind went to Lassie. He fought off his own thoughts. He would decide not to expect her to be there any more. But always, after he had crossed the schoolyard at the close of the day, his eyes would turn to the place beside the gate, despite his promises to himself never to expect her any more. She was never there, so things were not as they used to be.

But it was not only Lassie. Joe began to feel that many other "things" were not as they used to be. He felt that his parents now scolded him about matters that had never angered them in the old days. Sometimes, for instance, at meals, his mother would watch as he spooned the sugar into his tea. She would press her lips and sometimes now she would say:

"Now ye don't need to use all that sugar, Joe. It's—

it's—well, it isn't good for thee to eat so much sugar. It isn't healthy."

His mother seemed to be always so short tempered these days, another of the "things" that were not as they used to be.

One day when she had been setting out to do the weekend shopping, she had acted so strangely. And it was only because he had suggested that they have a roast of beef.

"Why don't we have a roast of beef for Sunday, Mother—and some Yorkshire pudding? We haven't had any for quite a time. Eigh, now I talk of it I'm rare hungry for some."

Once his mother and father had been proud of his appetite. They had laughed about it and joked about it and said he could eat enough for an elephant—and had always given him still more. But this time his mother had not laughed or even answered him. She had stood a moment, and then dropped her string market-bag, and without a word had run upstairs to the bedroom. And his father had stared at the stairs for a moment and then, without explanation, had jumped up and taken his cap and gone out, slamming the door behind him.

There were even more "things" that were not as they used to be. Often now when he came in, he would find his mother and father looking angrily at each other. They would stop talking the moment he arrived, but he could tell by their faces and their manner that they had been arguing.

Once, late at night, he had wakened and had heard them in the kitchen room below. It was not a pleasant drone of voices such as there used to be in the old days. The tones were puzzled and angry. And then, rising, Joe could hear the words his father was speaking:

"I tell thee I've walked my feet off for twenty miles

round here, and there's not a thing . . ."

Then the voice had quieted, and Joe heard his mother's voice, suddenly low and in a warm and comforting tone.

Many "things" were not as they used to be. In fact, so many of them that Joe felt nothing was as it used to be. And to him it all added up to one thing: Lassie.

When they had had Lassie, the home had been comfortable and warm and fine and friendly. Now that she was gone, nothing went right. So the answer was simple. If Lassie were only back again, then everything once more would be as it used to be.

Joe thought much about that. His mother had asked him to forget Lassie, but he could not. He could pretend to, and he could stop talking about her. But in his mind Lassie would always go on living.

He kept her living in his mind. He would sit at his desk at school and dream of her. He would think that perhaps some day—some day—like a dream come true, he would come out of school, and there she would be, sitting at the gate. He could see her just as if she were there, the sable and white of her coat gleaming in the sun, her eyes bright, her tipped ears thrust forward toward him so that she could hear the sound of a voice that tells a dog its master is near much sooner than its poor eyesight can. Her tail would move in welcome, and her mouth would be drawn back in the happy "laugh" of a dog.

Then they would race home—home—home—running through the village together, running gladly together.

So Joe dreamed. If he could not talk of his dog, he would never stop dreaming of her and hoping that some day . . .

The early, North-country English dusk was settling

as Joe came in. He saw his mother and father look up at him.

"What made thee so late?" his mother asked.

Her voice sounded hard and short. Joe felt that they had been talking again—talking as they did these days, with impatience to one another.

"I was kept after school," he said.

"What did tha do wrong to get kept for?"

"Teacher told me to sit down, and I didn't hear him."

His mother put her arms akimbo.

"What were tha doing, standing up?"

"I was looking out of the window."

"The window? What were tha looking out the window for?"

Joe stood silent. How could he explain to them? It would be better to say nothing.

"Tha hears thy mother?"

His father was standing angrily. Joe nodded.

"Well then, answer her. What were tha looking out the window for in school hours?"

"I couldn't help it."

"That's no answer. What does tha mean, tha couldn't help it?"

Joe felt the hopelessness of everything flooding over him—his father, who was so understanding usually, now angry at him. He felt the words beginning to race from his mouth.

"I couldn't help it. It was near four o'clock. It was time for her. I heard a dog barking. It sounded like her. I thought it was her, truly I did. I couldn't help it. I didn't think what I was doing, Mother. Truly. I was looking through the window to see if it were her, and I didn't hear Mr. Timms tell me to sit down. I thought it was Lassie—and she wasn't there."

Joe heard his mother's voice rising in impatience.

"Lassie, Lassie, Lassie! If I ever hear that name again. Is there never to be any peace and quiet in my home . . . ?"

Even his mother didn't understand!

Joe felt that most of all. If only his mother had understood!

The moment was too much for him. He felt hotness rising in his throat. He turned and ran to the door. He ran down the garden path into the deepening evening. He kept on running, up onto the moor.

Things would never be right again!

It was dark on the moor when Joe heard the sound of footsteps and his father's voice.

"Is that thee, Joe, lad?"

"Aye, Father!"

His father didn't seem to be angry any more. Joe suddenly felt comforted by the nearness of the tall, strong figure that loomed up beside him.

"Been walking, Joe?"

"Aye, Father," Joe said.

Joe knew it was hard for his father to "get talking" as he phrased it. It took his father such a long time to get the words going.

He felt his father's hand on his shoulder, and together they went along across the flat space. For a long time nothing was said. It was as if they were content to be together. Then Joe's father began.

"Now walking, Joe. That's a champion thing to do, isn't it, Joe?"

"Yes, Father."

His father nodded, and seemed quite happy with both his statement and his son's answer. He walked along freely, and Joe tried to stretch his legs so that he could match his father's firm, powerful stride. Together, unspeaking, they went up a rise, and then their feet rang on stone, and they were at the rocks. At last, by the edge of a slab, they sat. A half moon came from the rack of sky, and they could see the moor stretching away before them.

Joe saw his father put his short clay pipe in his mouth, and then absent-mindedly begin patting pocket after pocket, until his mind came to what he was doing. Then his hands ceased, and he began sucking his empty pipe.

"Haven't ye no tobacco, Father?" Joe asked.

"Why nay, lad. It's just—well, times being what they are—I've given up smoking."

Joe wrinkled his brow.

"Is it because we're poor, Father, and ye can't buy any tobacco?"

"Nay, now lad, we're not poor," Joe's father asserted, firmly. "It's just—times is not like they used to be and—well, anyhow, I smoked too much. It'll be good for ma health to stop for a while."

Joe sat in thought. Sitting there beside his father in the dimness, he knew that his father was "making it easy for him." He knew that his father was protecting him from worries that grownups had. Suddenly Joe felt grateful to his father, who was big and strong and who had followed him up to the moor to try to comfort him.

He put out his hand to touch his father's.

"You're not angry at me, are ye, Father?"

"Nay, Joe, a father can't get truly angry at his own lad—ever. It's just he wants him to understand how things are.

"That's what I wanted to say. Ye mustn't think we're over hard on thee. We don't want to be. It's just—well—back of it all, a chap's got to be honest, Joe. And never thee forget that, all thy life, no matter what. Ye've got to be honest."

Joe sat still. Now his father was talking, almost as if to himself, not gesticulating, but sitting perfectly still, speaking out toward the dim night.

"And sometimes, when a chap don't have much, Joe, he clings to being honest harder than ever—because that's all he does have left. At least, he stays honest. And there's a funny thing about honesty; there's no two ways about it. There's only one way about it. Honest is honest. D'ye see?"

Joe didn't quite understand what his father meant. But he did know that it must be something very important to his father, to make him go into such long sentences. His father usually said only "Aye" or "Nay," but now he was trying to talk. And somehow, Joe could feel the importance of what his father was trying to show him.

"It's like this, Joe. Seventeen year I worked in that Wellington Pit. Seventeen year, good time and bad time, full time and slack time, till she shut down for good. And a good collier I was, too, as any of my mates would vouch. In that seventeen year, Joe, butties I've had by the dozen, working alongside of me. But, my lad, there's not one can say that in all that time, Sam Carraclough ever took what wasn't his, nor spoke what wasn't true. Remember that, Joe. In all this West Riding there's not a man can stand up and say a Carraclough was ever mishonest.

"And that's what I mean by clinging to what ye've got. Honest is only one road. It can't be two. And ye're big enough to understand now that when ye've sold a chap something, and ye've taken his brass for it, and ye've spent it; well then, done's done. And Lassie was sold and that's all . . ."

"But, Father, she . . ."

"Now, now, Joe. Ye can't alter it. No matter how

many words tha says, tha can't alter it that she's sold, and we've taken the Duke's brass and spent it, and now she belongs to him."

For a while Sam Carraclough sat silent. Then he spoke again, as if to himself.

"And happen it were for the best at that. No two roads about it, she were getting hard to feed. A dog like that eats most as much as a good-grown child."

"We always fed her before."

"Aye, Joe, but ye've got to face things. Before, I were working. But now I'll have to face ye with it—I'm on the dole. And ye can't feed a dog right on that—ye can't feed a family right on it. So she's better off.

"Why look at it this way, lad. Ye wouldn't want Lassie going around looking peaked and pined and poorly. Ye wouldn't have her looking like the road some chaps round here keep their tykes, would thee?"

"We wouldn't pine her, Father. We could manage. I don't need to eat so much . . ."

"Now, Joe, that ain't the road to look at it."

They were silent, and then the man began again.

"Think on it this road, lad. Now ye're rare fond o' the tyke, aren't ye?"

"You know I am, Father."

"Well then, if that's so, tha should be truly happy because now she's so well off. Just think, Joe, now Lassie's got lots to eat—and a private kennel all to herself—and a fine big run—and everybody to care for her. Why, lad, she's just like a sort of princess living in her own palace and garden. That's it, she's just like a varritable princess now. Ain't that nice for her?"

"But Father, she'd be happier if . . ."

The man blew out his breath in exasperation.

"Eigh, Joe! There's no pleasing thee! Well then, I might as well let thee have it straight from the shoulder. Tha might as well put Lassie clean out o' thy mind, because tha's never off to see her no more."

"But she might get away . . ."

"Nay, lad, nay! She's run away her last time, and that were once too often. She'll never run—never any more!"

Joe forced the words from him.

"What did they do to her?"

"Well, last time I took her back, the Duke got angry at me and Hynes and the whole lot. And I got mad at him, for I don't owe him a penny, Duke or no Duke, and I said if she got away again, he'd not see her no more, and he said if she ever got away again I was welcome to her, but he'd see she didn't. So he's taken her with him up to his place in Scotland. He's off to get her ready for the shows. Hynes has gone up wi' her and half a dozen more likely show dogs. But after the shows, she goes back to Scotland, and she's never to be kept down here in Yorkshire any more.

"So there she stays for good, so it's good-bye, and good luck to her. She's not coming home no more. Now I weren't off to tell thee this, but it's happen best tha should know. So there it is, and put it in thy pipe and smoke it.

"Now what can't be helped in this life must be endured, Joe lad. So bide it like a man, and let's never say another word about it as long as we live—especially in front o' thy mother."

Then Joe found himself stumbling down the path from the rocky crags, and they were going over the moor. His father did not comfort him but merely walked along, still sucking his empty pipe. It was not until they were near to the village and could see the windows shining that the man spoke again.

"Just afore we go in, Joe," he said, "I want thee to think on thy mother. Tha's growing up, and tha must try to be like a man wit' her and understand her.

"Now women, Joe, they're not like men. They have to stay home, women do, and manage as best they can. And what they haven't got—well, they've got to spend time in wishing for.

"And when things don't go right, well, they have to take it out in talk and give a man hot words. But if a man's really got any gumption, he gives 'em that much. For he knows a woman really doesn't mean owt by it when she natters and nags and lets her tongue go. So tha mustn't mind it when thy mother talks hard at me, or if she sometimes snaps at thee. She's got a lot to put up with these days, and it tries her patience.

"So it's us that has to be patient, Joe. Thee and me. And then—some day—well, happen things'll pick up again and times'll be better for all of us. D'ye understand, lad?"

Joe's father reached over and pressed his son's arm quickly, in a gesture of encouragement.

"Yes, Father," Joe said.

He stood for a while looking at the lighted village.

"Father. Is it very far to Scotland?"

The man stood, his head sunk on his broad chest. He breathed deeply and sadly.

"A long, long way, Joe. Much farther than tha'll ever travel, I'd say. A long, long road."

Then sadly, they went together down to the village.

A Captive in the Highlands

It is, as Sam Carraclough had said to his son, "a long, long way" from the village of Greenall Bridge in Yorkshire to the Duke of Rudling's estate up in the Scottish Highlands. Much farther than you would wish to walk.

To get there you would go almost directly north—first out across the moors and the flatlands of Yorkshire. Winding east, you would go past wild land, then through rich farming districts. If you were going by train, you would soon look through the windows at the right and see the North Sea, shining down beneath the high cliffs. There would be on your left the spires of ancient cities, and then the pall of grime over the industrial centers of Durham, where the great shipways stand along the river mouths, and the coal goes pouring by train to the docks of the seaports.

Dark night falls early as you travel, for this land is in a high latitude where the sun sinks early and rises late. But your train would go on and on, screaming in the darkness as it raced over the bridges, crossing rivers, crossing at last the Tweed River, which means that you are leaving England behind.

Through the night the train would race on, clattering past the industrial towns of Lowland Scotland, where the furnaces and forges glow brighter in the darkness than by day. During the night your train would go over mighty bridges, carrying you across the very wide river mouths that the Scottish people call "firths."

In the morning your train would still be racing, only now the country would have changed. There would be no more cities belching smoke. Instead you would see the beautiful Scottish land that the poets have sung about for centuries, the blue mountains and green-bordered lakes, and the rolling land where the shepherds watch their flocks.

On and on the train would go, and the land would become wilder and wilder, the hills more rugged, the lochs more closely enclosed by woodlands. It would be lonelier and lonelier—now great expanses of heatherland where men are seldom seen, where the deer still roam. On and on you would go, right up to the tip of the northern land.

And there, in that farthermost point, is the great Scottish estate of the Duke of Rudling, the frowning stone house that looks out over the sea toward the Shetland Islands—those strange rock-bound dots of land where life is so hard and the weather so severe that nature seems to have adjusted most forms of life so that they may survive; where the horses and dogs have become tiny, but also extraordinarily sturdy, so that they may continue to live in that stern land with its stern climate.

And there, far away in that northern land, was Lassie's new home. There she was fed and tended carefully. The food she was given was of the best. Each day she was combed and brushed and manicured and taught to stand in a perfect position so that some day soon she might go to the big shows and win more renown for the Duke of Rudling and his kennels.

She submitted patiently to all the handling of Hynes, as if she knew there were no use making any protest, but each day, just before four o'clock in the afternoon, something waked in her, and the training of a lifetime called her. She would tear against the wires of her pen or dash at the fence and try to leap it.

She had not forgotten.

In the clear, healthy coolness of the Highland air, the Duke of Rudling rode down the trail. Beside him, on her frisky cob, rode Priscilla. Her horse arched its neck and bucketed gaily.

"Hands," the Duke boomed. "That's what does it. Collect her now lightly. Good hands."

Priscilla smiled. For her grandfather considered himself such an authority on all animals that he could not ride without keeping up a stream of admonitions. But actually he was quite proud of Priscilla's riding, and she knew it.

"That's what nature gave you hands and legs for," he roared. "Legs to push a horse forward, hands to collect him. Legs and hands does it!"

The Duke sat erect and proceeded to give an example, but his sturdy gray hack ambled along patiently with no change of gait or carriage. Truly, if the Duke had had his way, despite his age, he would have gone riding on the most spirited saddle horses available; but his entire family, in what amounted to an alliance, had conspired to limit him to the safe and uninspired hack that he now rode. Priscilla knew that too, so she nodded her head as if his plodding horse had just broken into proud carriage and mincing gait.

"Oh, I understand now what you mean, Grandfather," she said.

The Duke expanded his chest happily. For, in truth, he was happy. In his old age he found little to delight him more thoroughly than his granddaughter, and he could wish for nothing finer than these days during which they rode or walked about his northern estate.

"Just look at this weather! Marvelous! Wonderful!"

He shouted it with an air of proud ownership, as if
he alone, the Duke of Rudling, were responsible for
the tang in the air and the gentle warmth of the sun.

"All summer here," he announced gladly. "All summer. Then in autumn, back to Yorkshire. Then we'll
have some more good times together."

"But in the autumn I'm going away to school. I'll be
far away in Switzerland, Grandfather!"

"Switzerland!"

The Duke roared the word in such thunderous tones
that Priscilla's cob skipped nimbly a half dozen feet
sidewise.

"But I've got to go to school, Grandfather."

"Poppycock," the Duke thundered. "Sending girls to
school in foreign lands—teaching them to jabber away
in foreign languages like monkeys. Never could understand why they have such things as foreign languages—or if they have 'em, why anybody with any
sense should wish to jabber 'em. Look at me. English is
good enough for me. Never spoke a word of any other
language in all my life, and I've got along well enough,
haven't I?"

"But you wouldn't want me to grow up uneducated,
would you, Grandfather?"

"Uneducated! You're educated enough. All this
modern nonsense isn't education—teaching a girl to
jibber-jabber away in some sort of senseless language
that only a foreigner knows how to understand. Modern nonsense, that's what I call it!

"In my day, we educated people properly."

"What's properly, Grandfather?"

"Teach you how to run a house, that's what. In my
day, girls were brought up to do their duty—run a
home properly. Nowadays they fill their heads full of
nonsense. Pooh—this modern generation. They grow

up impertinent. Always contradicting their elders. No respect for age, that's what. You contradict me—well, I forbid it. I won't have any more impertinence! For you are impertinent, aren't you?"

"Yes, Grandfather."

"Yes? Yes? You dare say yes right to my face?"

"I had to, Grandfather. You just told me not to contradict you, and if I said no, then I would be contradicting you, wouldn't I?"

"Hrrumph!" the Duke said. "Hrrumph!"

Then he brushed his long white moustache triumphantly, as if he had won a battle. He looked down at his granddaughter, with her long flaxen hair tumbling from underneath the pert riding hat and cascading down onto her jersey-clad shoulders. He coughed and snorted and flourished his moustache again, and then he smiled and nodded his head.

"You're an impertinent baggage," he said. "But there's some hope for you. You know, you're just like I was when I was your age. You're like me, that's what you are. You take after me—the only one of the family that does! So there's some hope for you."

The horses clattered into the cobbled stableyard, and the Duke puffed as the groom ran out to take them.

"Don't hold his head, man," he shouted at the groom. "I hate to have anybody hold a horse's head while I'm dismounting. I can dismount perfectly without any help from anyone."

Fussing and fuming in his bad-tempered way, the Duke stood while Priscilla slackened the girth of her pony and led him toward the stall.

"That's right," he shouted, in what was his most agreeable tone. "No girl should be allowed to ride a horse who doesn't know how to feed and saddle 'em. If you don't know how yourself, you'll never be able to tell anyone else how to do it properly."

Thus, in a good temper, the old man walked with his granddaughter along by the stables toward the great house. It was as they came by the low, stone building that Priscilla halted. For by the building were the runs for the dogs. In each one a dog leaped and barked a bedlam—except in one pen. In that pen was a beautiful tricolor collie. And she did not bark or leap. Instead she stood, her head turned to the south. She gazed into space.

And that was the dog Priscilla saw.

"What is it? What's up now?" the Duke said testily.

"That collie. Why is she chained, Grandfather?"

The Duke started and fixed his attention on the dog. For a second he was still, then it seemed as if some explosion had taken place in him. His voice rose so that the stables and the kennels thundered.

"Hynes! Hynes! Where is that man hiding? Where is he?"

"Coming, sir. Coming," came the voice of Hynes, as the kennelman trotted in from the other direction.

"Yes, sir. 'Ere, sir."

The Duke whirled.

"Well, don't sneak up behind me like that," the Duke bellowed. "What's that dog doing on a chain?"

"Well, I 'ad to put 'er on a chain, sir," said Hynes, dropping the "h's" at the beginning of certain words and putting them in where they did not belong at the beginning of others. "She tears and scratches the wire away. I've mended it a dozen times, but every afternoon she's at it again. You told me to be sure and . . ."

"I never said a chain! No dog of mine goes on a chain—understand that?"

"Yes, sir."

"Then don't forget it. No dog—ever!"

The Duke whirled in anger, almost treading on Priscilla's toes. He looked down on her as she tugged his sleeve.

"Grandfather, she doesn't look at all well. She's had no exercise. Couldn't she come walking with us? She's so pretty!"

The Duke shook his head.

"Couldn't do that, m'dear. She'd never get in shape."

"In shape?"

"Yes. Going to show her. She's a champion. If we let her run wild with us she'd get—oh, burrs in her coat, and her leggings would get torn and spoiled. Couldn't have that, you know."

"But she ought to have some exercise, shouldn't she?"

The two of them stared at the dog behind the wire. Lassie stood, ignoring them as if she were a queen and they were beings so far beneath her that she could not see them.

The Duke rubbed his chin.

"Yes. She could do with a bit more exercise, I should say. Hynes!"

"Yes, sir?"

"She needs walking. You see she gets a good walk every day."

"She'll try to run away, sir."

"Put a leash on her, you idiot! You walk with her yourself. See she gets exercise. I want that dog in perfect condition."

"Yes, sir."

The Duke and Priscilla turned to the house. Hynes watched their backs. When they were out of sight he put on his cap savagely. He drew the back of his hand across his mouth, and then turned to the dog.

"So ye 'ave to 'ave a walk, do ye, milady?" he said. "Well, I'll walk ye. Not 'arf I won't."

But the dog paid no attention to his voice. She stood at the end of the chain, still gazing before her—gazing to the south.

Freedom Again at Last

It was Lassie's time sense that did it—that curious sense in an animal that tells exactly what time of the day it is.

For had it been any other part of the day, Lassie might have followed her lifetime training to obey a spoken order and returned to Hynes as he bid her. But she did not.

It had been while on one of the newly ordered walks, with Lassie going along obediently at Hynes's heel. The leash was about Lassie's neck, but she neither tugged ahead on it nor lingered behind so that it tugged at her. She was going as a well-trained dog should go, close at the left heel so that her head almost touched Hynes's knee.

Everything was orderly as could be wished, except that Hynes had not forgotten his resentment about being forced to take exercise himself so that Lassie could be kept in good fettle. He wanted to get back to his tea—and he also wanted to show Lassie "who was boss."

And so, quite needlessly, he suddenly tugged on the leash.

"Come along wiv yer, will yer?" he snapped.

Lassie felt the sudden tug on her neck and hesitated. She was only slightly puzzled. She knew from long training that she was doing exactly what was expected of her. Obviously, though, this man expected something else. She wasn't sure what it was.

In the moment of indecision, she slackened her pace. Almost gladly Hynes noted this. He turned and yanked at the leash.

"Come on, now. Come on when I tell yer," he shouted.

Lassie backed away from the threatening tone. Hynes yanked again. Lassie did what any dog will do: she braced herself for the tug and lowered her head.

Hynes tugged harder. The leash slipped up over Lassie's head.

She was free!

In that split second, Hynes acted according to his nature—but not according to his own knowledge as a dog-man. He jumped to grab Lassie. It was exactly the wrong thing to do. For instinctively she jumped away to elude him.

Hynes's action had done only one thing. It had shown Lassie clearly that she wanted to keep away from him. Had he spoken to her in an ordinary manner, she might have come to him. In fact, if he had just ordered her to heel, she might have followed him back to the kennel held by nothing more than her trained habits of obedience to man.

Hynes was enough of a dog-man, however, to understand this—to see that he had made a bad mistake, that if he moved menacingly again he might frighten the dog even more. So he began to do what he should have done in the first place.

"Here, Lassie. Come here," he said.

Lassie stood in indecision. One instinct told her to obey. But the memory of the tugging and the sudden leap at her was too fresh.

Hynes saw that. He lifted his voice in a high, whee-dling tone that he thought might be alluring.

"Nice Lassie. Nice dog," he chanted. "Nice dog—now stay there. Don't you move, now. Stay there."

He half knelt, snapping his fingers to hold the dog's attention. Imperceptibly, inch by inch, he crept nearer.

"Stand still, now," Hynes ordered.

The lifetime of training that Sam Carraclough had given Lassie seemed to have its effect now. For even though Lassie disliked Hynes, she had been schooled thoroughly to obey human beings who spoke words of command to her.

But another lifetime impulse also stirred in her—although only faintly. It was the time sense.

Dimly, mistily, it began to waken in her. She did not know it or reason it or think it clearly as a man would. It began to grow in her faintly. It was only a weak stir-ring.

It was time—time to—time to . . .

She watched Hynes creeping nearer. Her head lifted a trifle.

It was time—time to—time to go . . .

Hynes edged himself nearer. In another second he would be near enough to grab the dog—to sink his fin-gers into the wealth of heavy mane and hang on until he could slip the guardian leash over her head again.

Lassie watched him. The stirring was becoming plainer.

It was time—time to go for . . .

Hynes gathered himself. As if sensing it, Lassie moved. Quickly she backed away two paces from the crawling man. She wanted to be free.

"Drat you," Hynes exploded.

As if he realized this mistake, he began all over again.

"Nice Lassie, now. Stand still, there. Stand still. Stay there."

Lassie was not listening to him now, however. With only a small part of her senses she was watching the man edging nearer. All the rest of her was increasingly intent upon the sitrring that was becoming clearer and clearer. She wanted time. She felt somehow that if this man reached her, she would be disappointed once more.

She stepped back again. And just at that moment Hynes leaped. Lassie dodged aside.

Angrily Hynes stood erect. He walked toward her, speaking soothing words. Lassie backed away. Always she kept the same distance between Hynes and herself—the distance an animal knows so well—the distance that places it beyond the sudden reach of an enemy.

Her instinct was saying:

"Keep away from him. Do not let him reach you. For there is something—something else. It is time— time to go—time to go for the . . ."

And then, suddenly, in that second, Lassie knew. She knew as surely and irrevocably as the hands of a clock that point to five minutes to four.

It was time to go for the boy!

She wheeled and began trotting away—trotting as if she had but to go a few hundred yards. There was nothing to tell her that the rendezvous she would keep was hundreds of miles and scores of days away. There was only the plain, unadorned knowledge of a duty to be done. And she was going to do it as best she could.

But now, behind her, she heard Hynes. He was running, shouting. She broke from her trot into a gentle lope. She was not afraid. It was as if she knew surely that this two-footed creature could never catch up with her. She didn't even need to put on speed. Her thrown-back ears told her how near Hynes was. Then, too, dogs, like most other animals, have their eyes set much more at the side of their heads than do human beings, and thus are able to see behind them with only the slightest turn of the head.

Lassie did not seem to worry about Hynes. She just kept on going at a steady lope, down the path, over the lawn.

For a second, Hynes's heart leaped with hope. Perhaps, he thought, Lassie would head back to the kennels.

But the kennels, where she had been chained and penned, were not a home for Lassie. They were a hated place. And Hynes's hope died as he saw the collie turn down the gravel path toward the front gate.

Hynes's heart gave a leap again. The gate was always closed, and the walls about the "home" part of the estate were tall, frowning granite ones. Perhaps he could corner her yet.

Priscilla and her grandfather rode up the road from the fishing village and halted by the iron gate to the estate.

"I'll open it, Grandfather," the girl said.

She slipped lightly from her saddle as the Duke began mumbling in protest. But Priscilla knew she could dismount and mount again much more easily than her grandfather. For despite all protests, he was an old man, and climbing up into the saddle of even the quietest horse was a task accompanied by much fuming and puffing and groaning.

Linking the reins over her bent arm, the girl drew back the bolt. Then putting her weight against the wrought-iron structure, she swung it slowly back on its hinges.

It was only at this moment that she heard the noise.

Looking up the path, she saw Hynes. He was racing toward her. Before him was the beautiful collie. And Hynes was shouting:

"Close that gate, Miss Priscilla! Close that gate! That collie's loose. Don't let 'er get out! Close the gate!"

Priscilla looked about her. Before her was the great gate. All she needed to do was swing it shut and Lassie would be trapped inside the home grounds.

She looked up at her grandfather. He was unaware of all the stir. His deaf ears had not caught the high shoutings of Hynes.

Priscilla began to pull the gate. For a second she swung her weight back on it. She half heard her grandfather beginning to roar in puzzled protest. But she forgot that, as she saw again a certain picture in her mind.

It was the picture of a village boy just a little taller than herself, standing beside the meshed wire of a run, saying to his dog: "Bide here forever and leave us be—and don't never come home no more." And she knew then that while the boy was saying it, every sense and part of him was crying out to say just the opposite.

So she stood, seeing the picture in her mind, listening to the words again as if they were spoken plainly. And still she had not closed the gate.

Her grandfather was still fuming, knowing something was happening that his aged senses could not grasp. Hynes was still screaming:

"Close that gate, Miss Priscilla. Close it!"

Priscilla stood in a moment of indecision, then quickly began swinging the gate wide open. A blur flashed past her knees and when Priscilla looked down the road, she saw the dog going at a steady gait as if it knew it had a long, long way to go. So Priscilla lifted her hand.

"Good-bye, Lassie," she said softly. "Good-bye and—good luck!"

On his horse sat the Duke, not looking down the road at the collie, but staring at his granddaughter.

"Well, drat my buttons," he breathed. "Drat my buttons."

A Long Journey's Beginning

It was growing dusk as Lassie came down the dusty
road. Now she trotted more slowly, and there was indecision in her gait. She halted and then turned back
toward the direction from which she had come. She
lifted her head, for she was badly puzzled.

Now the pull of the time sense was leaving her. A
dog knows nothing of maps and of distances as a man
does. By this time Lassie should have met the boy, and
they should be on their way home again—home to eat.

It was time to eat. The years of routine told Lassie
that. Back in the kennels there would be a platter of
fine beef and meal set before her. But back in the kennel also was a chain that made a dog a prisoner.

Lassie stood in indecision, and then another sense
began to waken. It was the homing sense—one of the
strongest of all instincts in animals. And home was not
the kennel she had left. Home was a cottage where she
lay on the rug before the fire, where there was warmth
and where voices and hands caressed her. Now that
she was lost, that was where she would go.

Lifting her head again, as the desire for her true
home woke in her, she scented the breeze as if asking
directions. Then, without hesitation, she struck down
the road to the south. Do not ask any human being to
explain how she should know this. Perhaps, thousands
upon thousands of years ago, before man "educated"

his brain, he too had the same homing sense; but if he had it, it is gone now. Not with all his brain development can man tell how a bird or an animal can be crated, taken miles away in darkness, and when released, strike straight back toward its home. Man only knows that animals can do what he can neither do himself nor explain.

And in Lassie there was no hesitation. Her senses were now aware of a great satisfaction, for there was peace inside her being. She was going home. She was happy.

There was no one to tell her, and no way for her to learn that what she was attempting was almost in the realm of the impossible—that there were hundreds of miles to go over wild land—a journey that would baffle most men going on foot.

A man could buy food on the way, but what coin has a dog to pay for food? No coin except the love of his master. A man can read signs on the road—but a dog must go blindly, on instinct. A man would know how to cross the great lochs that stretch from east to west almost across the entire country, barring the way of any animal going south. And how could a dog know that she was valuable, and that in villages and towns lived hundreds of men of keen eye, who would wish to capture her for that reason?

There were so many things that a dog could not know, but by experience a dog might learn.

Happily Lassie set out. The journey had begun.

In the last of the long Northern twilight two men sat outside their cottage. It was like the other cottages which lined the village's old, narrow street. The cottage walls were thick with the whitewash coating of years.

The elder man, clad in rough homespun, lit his pipe carefully and as it drew freely lifted his head. He watched the puffs of smoke eddying away in the still evening air. Then he felt the sudden clasp of the younger man's hand on his arm.

"Wullie, see yonder!"

The older man looked where the other was pointing. He sat for some time until his eyes saw more plainly in the evening. It was a dog coming toward them.

The younger man, who wore leggings and a corduroy suit, stood up. "Looks like a good 'un, Wullie," he said.

"Aye, Geordie—a fine collie."

Their eyes followed the dog as she trotted near. Then the younger man stirred.

"Havers, Wullie. It looks like that fine collie belongin' tae the laird. It is! I'll sweer on it. I saw it two days back when I were up chinnin' to McWheen aboot the salmon season. It'll be escaped, no doot . . ."

"Och, and then there'll be . . ."

"Aye, a rewarrrd for the mon that finds . . ."

"Losh, aye!"

"Hi!"

The younger man flung this last cry over his shoulder, for he was dashing out into the street. He barred the dog's way.

"Here, lass," he called. "Here, lass!" He patted his hand on his knee in a gesture of friendliness.

Lassie looked up at him. Her ear had caught the sound that was almost her name: lass. Had the man walked toward her, she might have let him place his hand on her. But he moved too quickly. Suddenly Lassie was reminded of Hynes. She veered slightly, and without altering her trot, ran past him. The man dove at her. Her muscles flexed, and, like a football star, she put on a spurt that upset his timing. She loped a few steps and then went back to the purposeful trot. But the man raced after her down the village street. Lassie quickened her pace again and broke into a steady gallop. The more he chased her, the more firmly it was becoming fixed in her mind that she must not let any human being put his hands on her. To chase a dog is merely to teach it to run away.

When the Scot saw that he had no chance of catching the dog by speed, he halted and picked up a loose stone. He thought he could hurl it ahead of Lassie, so that the sound of it falling might head her off and turn her back toward him. He drew back his arm and threw.

The aim was bad. The stone fell almost at Lassie's shoulder. Even as it was falling, she changed her gallop as a well-trained polo pony does, leading with the other forefoot. She veered away into the ditch. Belly-close, she went at an amazing speed. There was a gap in a hedge. She faded through it and shot away from the road up into the bleak back-country.

Once there, she turned south again and went back to the steady trot.

But now Lassie had learned one thing. She must keep away from men. For some reason that she could not understand, their hands were against her. Their voices now were rough and angry. They shouted and threw things. There was menace in men. Therefore, she must keep away from them. The thought stayed firmly with her. Lassie had learned her first lesson in the first day.

That first night Lassie traveled steadily. Never before in her five years of life had she been out alone at night. So there was no training to help, only her instinct.

But the instinct within her was keen and alert. Steadily she followed a path over the heather-clad land. The path filled her with a warm satisfaction, for it was going south. She trotted along it confidently and surely.

At last she reached a rise and then, in the hollow below, she saw the dim shapes of farm buildings. She halted, abruptly, with her ears thrown forward and her nose trembling. Her magnificently acute senses read the story of the habitation below as clearly as a human being might read a book.

She read of horses standing in the barns, of sheep, of another dog, of food, of humans. She started down the slope warily. The smell of food was pleasant, and she had gone a long time without eating. But she knew she must be cautious, for men were there, too. And it was becoming fixed in her mind that she must keep away from them. She trotted down the path.

Then there came a sudden challenging bark of the other dog. She could hear him racing toward her. She stood, waiting. Perhaps he was friendly.

But he was not. He came tearing up the path, his mane erect, his ears flat. Lassie crouched to meet him. As he sprang, she stepped aside. He turned, giving loud voice in hysterical rage. His tones were saying: "This is my home—you are an intruder. It is my home, and I will defend it."

Then, from the farm below, came the muffled voice of a man. "What is it, Tammie? Sic 'em up!"

At the sound of the human voice, Lassie wheeled. She trotted away. This was not *her* home. She was an outcast here.

The rough-coated shepherd charged as she loped away, worrying at her flanks. She turned quickly, her lips curling. As if that menace were enough, the other dog drew back.

Steadily she trotted on. The farm was soon left be-

hind. She went over the wild country, following the animal paths. Finally she scented water. She found the
small, cold stream and lapped greedily. The sky was
graying in the east. She looked about her.

By a rock she scratched gently with her forepaw.
She turned around three times and then curled herself
up. Behind her was the protecting overhang of the
rock. Her head faced outward. Now, even though she
slept, her nose and ears would warn her of any ap-
proaching danger.

She put her head on her paw and sighed loudly.

Early the next morning Lassie was on her way
again. She went steadily at a swinging trot that drove at
the miles. Her muscles paced with inexorable rhythm,
uphill, downhill. She did not pause or hesitate. Whenever a path ran to the south, she followed it. If it
veered away, she left it, keeping to animal paths
through the dense heather and brush.

When a path led toward a town or a farm, she shied
away, circling the habitations to keep away from man.
So at the places where men lived she went warily, instinctively keeping under cover, gliding like a ghost under the shadow of thicket and brush, taking advantage
of any woodland.

For the most part her ground lay uphill, for ahead of
her was a range of blue mountains. Unerringly she
headed for the lowest dip where there would be a pass.
As the day wore on and she gained higher ground and
higher, the sky became overcast. The clouds looked
leaden.

Then suddenly there was a flash, and thunder
pealed. Lassie hesitated and whined in a quick, querulous tone. She was frightened. It is little use to blame a
dog for having fear. A dog has so many braveries that

its few fears do not cancel them out. And truth to tell, there are few collies that can stand thunder and lightning.

Many dogs do not mind such noise. There are breeds of hunting dogs that are never so happy as when a gun is sounded. But not a collie. It seems as if this breed, having worked so long as man's companion, has learned that such sharp, savage sounds may mean hurt. And the crack of a gun will send most collies running for cover. Other foes they will face, but not the unknown danger of noise.

So Lassie hesitated. The rolling peals of thunder echoed through the mountains, and the torrents of rain lashed down in one of the wild storms of north Scotland. For a long time she fought her fear, but at last it was too much. She trotted to a place on the boulder-strewn pass where overhanging ledges made a dry cave. There she crouched, pressing herself back against the rock as the thunder drummed and echoed.

But if she had halted her journey, it was not for long. As the storm went muttering away down the mountain range, Lassie got to her feet. For a second she stood, head high, questing the breeze. Then again she started, going in that long, swinging trot.

The rain and the splashed earth now made the beautiful expanse of her coat tarnished and spotted. But she kept on going steadily, going to the south.

The Fight for Existence

For the first four days, Lassie traveled without pause, resting only briefly during the nights. The urge to travel south burned in her like a fever, and nothing could replace it.

On the fifth day a new demand began to gnaw at her senses. It was the call of hunger. The command to travel had blotted it out at first, but now it was insistent.

She had had no trouble in finding streams to quench her thirst, but the problem of getting food was one far removed from her protected life. From her first memory, food had never been her responsibility. At stated times it was provided for her. Man put it down before her in a platter. She had been taught carefully that that was her portion, and she must never eat any food that lay elsewhere. Year after year, that lesson had been driven into her. Food was not her responsibility. Man provided it.

But now, suddenly, the training and conditioning of a lifetime were useless. There was no man to put down a pan of food each afternoon. And yet this aristocratic animal must learn to exist.

Lassie found the way. She did not reason it out as a human being would. Human beings have imagination—they can picture events and circumstances before they meet them. Dogs cannot do this; they must wait blindly until the circumstance faces them and then do their best to meet it.

Yet how could Lassie meet this new problem? She had not the brain of a man to reason it out. Nor could she base her conduct on the past experience of others of her kind, in the way humans do. A young child does not have to undergo many dangerous experiences in life to find out the result, for his parents and other older persons can tell him from their acquired knowledge what will result in such a case. No animal can pass on its acquired knowledge to its young in this way. Every animal must meet each new experience as if it had never faced his kind before in the history of the world. How then should Lassie learn how to feed herself?

She had that quality that is in animals, which man perhaps had once, but has no longer: instinct.

With instinct, and the lessons of their own past experiences, animals manage to arrive at conclusions that man reaches by his reasoning power.

It was instinct that drove Lassie daily in one direction. It was past experience that taught her to be wary of human beings. It was instinct that told her how to keep out of their sight—to follow the low ground of ravines, to glide belly-low on the skylines. Instinct taught her to find food.

On the fifth day as she went along, traveling at her fast, swinging trot, her senses began to warn her. She halted in the half-beaten animal track through the wild heather and with head forward stood transfixed, her eyes, her ears, her nose reading the signs that came so faintly that a human being would have been insensible to them.

It was her sense of smell that deciphered the puzzle first. There was a warm, thick smell—the smell of food.

The habit of a lifetime impelled Lassie to run toward it openly. But instinct overruled habit. She dropped to a crouch, and with body low began to creep up-wind toward the smell. Silently she moved through the heather, edging nearer and nearer. And then, suddenly, on the path she saw what her nose had warned her of. Coming down the path, his snakelike body undulating, was a weasel. His head was lifted high, and by his side he dragged the freshly killed body of a rabbit. His game was much bigger than himself, yet the powerfully built killer was dragging it along at a surprising speed. Then his senses warned him, too, and he whirled in defiance. Dropping his quarry, he turned to face the menace. His savage, white teeth were bared, and he gave a shrill cry that sounded like one of defiant rage.

Lassie, with head low, gazed at him. She had never seen such an animal before. Nor was there in her breeding the instinct of the terrier kind, which will dash more quickly than thought of man at any form of rodent life. She was a working-dog breed, a dog of peace—and yet instinct drove her on.

Slowly the ruff on her neck rose. The lips curled back from her teeth. Her ears lay flat against her head. She gathered her hindquarters under her.

But at the second she sprang, as if knowing the precise moment when that would be, the screaming weasel flashed aside. With lightning rapidity, he wove his way through the tangled heather, going silently, swiftly, flowing like water. Lassie whirled to look for him, but her senses were drawn to something else—the warm, blood smell of the rabbit that lay on the path.

For a long time she regarded it. She came nearer, bending her head warily, as if ready to spring away. For, though the blood smell of food was there, the scent of the weasel still lingered, too. Carefully her nose came nearer and nearer until it touched the fresh-

ly killed quarry. She drew back and walked around
it. Then she came near, bent her head, and picked up
the game. She lifted her head again and waited.

It was as if, in that wild land, far from all human
beings, she was expecting the sudden call of the master: "No, Lassie! Drop it! Drop it!"

But no sound came.

She stood indecisively for almost a half minute, and
then it was over. Carrying the rabbit, she trotted along.
She quested to right and left as she went. Then she saw
what she wanted—a thick tangle of gorse that made a
sort of den. She walked to it, coiled herself close so
that she was protected on three sides. She dropped to
the ground, letting the rabbit fall before her. She
smelled it again. It smelled good. It was food.

After that she had a newly acquired sense. She had
learned the smell of rabbit. Instinct told her the rest.
As she traveled along, whenever her keen nose told her
of the nearness of game, she became a hunter. She
scouted and ran and caught it, and she ate. It was the
sensible law of nature. She did not kill wantonly as
man often does. She killed to live, and no more.

Such food was just sufficient to sustain life, but that
was all. Now there were no keen eyes to watch Lassie,
to note her weight, to look at the color of her gums, to
eye the quality of her coat. There was no one to say:

"She's off a couple of pounds—give her a little more
beef liver in her dinner!"

"She doesn't seem quite up to snuff—better start giving her a bowl of milk in the morning. Ye might just
drop a raw egg in it if she'll take it!"

"Hmmm—I don't quite like the color of her gums. I
think she'd better have a spoonful of cod liver oil once
a day. That'll bring her up to condition!"

Not now all those cares for a royal dog that lies of
nights in a dry kennel. Instead it was a dog with

pinched, lean flanks; with coat blotched and torn; with petticoats and tail matted with burrs. But it was still a dog that had lived a life under loving care, so that it had known no sickness. And those years of care were telling now. For the frame was rugged and the muscles strong, and they drove along, mile after mile each day.

And the heart was gallant and the instinct was true. So the dog went, day after day, steadily south in the Highlands, over bracken and heather, through hill-land and plain, through stream and woodland—ever going steadily, always south.

What a Painter Saw

The time was turning to the deepness of summer. Leslie Freeth lay back lazily in the bow of the rowboat. He puffed his pipe contentedly and watched the smoke go evenly in the cool morning air, drifting back to where McBane methodically pulled at the oars.

"It'd be better if I sat in the back, Mr. McBane," he said.

"Nay, she trims better, I've told ye, Mr. Freeth. She's a verra peculiar boat," the oarsman said.

Freeth puffed evenly and gave himself up to the day. There was no reasoning with these hard-headed Scots. Yet if McBane wanted him in the bow . . .

His eyes took in the glory of the Scottish landscape, and Freeth was happy. The lochs—happy hunting ground of the British fishermen—meant something else to Leslie Freeth. They are the places whose beauty, long treasured by the Scotsmen, is also a magnet to English painters. And Leslie Freeth was one of those who never tired of the everlasting change of light and shadow that moved about the wide waters and the purpling hills. Each summer he came again, to paint and to resume earthy contact with the McBanes, who dourly welcomed him back to their cottage and gave him studio room in their fine stone barn.

So, content with the day, he lay back in the bow until the boat grated on the shingle of a small island.

Mechanically he helped McBane unload the paraphernalia, the easel, the canvases, the metal paint boxes. He set up the canvas and the folding chair. He cocked his head to one side and regarded the unfinished painting.

"Weel, I'll be back for ye at the noon," McBane said.

"All right, Mr. McBane. I'll be several hours on this. How d'you think it's coming?"

McBane walked heavily to a position of vantage and, shutting one eye, began cocking his head from side to side. Throughout the long winters, at the small inn by the loch, McBane would argue for hours if need be that his Mr. Freeth was one of Britain's greatest landscapists, before whom all the Dutch and the French school would have bowed—if only they had been still alive to do so. But in the artist's presence, McBane never let his undoubtedly prejudiced opinion show for an instant.

"Weel, sin' ye're asking me, I would say she's a wee bit on the gaudy side. T' watter's a bit too violent, and losh, but I never saw the sky that color—and yer clouds is verra startlin'. But I don't doubt she's fine elsewheres."

Leslie Freeth smiled. He was used to McBane's criticisms. Moreover, he really valued them, for the dour Scotsman had a good eye and a sound appreciation of his fair-faced land. So Freeth nodded, his eyes going from his canvas to the landscape, back and forth. He was thinking how still it all was. Not a movement anywhere, except the gentle lap of the water that slapped at the bottom of the rowboat down by the shore. Not a movement—except . . .

He shaded his eyes. "See that, Mr. McBane—a deer?"

The Scotsman glanced at Freeth's outstretched arm

pointing. His own eyes sought the shore of the
northern mainland. The heavy, sandy eyebrows lowered as if they would shield the gray-blue eyes below
them.

"A deer?" the artist repeated his question.

McBane shook his head without speaking. His eyes,
used to the outdoors, were keener than the Englishman's.

"Weel, I never," he said finally.

"What is it?"

"A dog," the old man said.

He shaded his eyes with his hand. The artist did the
same.

"So it is. I can see now."

Now that he was satisfied, Freeth made as if to turn
to his painting, but the older man still gazed steadily.
His attention brought the artist back to steady staring.

"A collie," McBane said. "Now what would it be
doing . . ."

"Oh, probably one from somewhere around—a farm
dog."

The Scotsman shook his head. Gazing steadily, he
saw the animal come to the water's edge and wade in
several feet. Then it backed away, ran along the bank
several yards, and tried again. It kept repeating this, as
if at some new spot it would find the water had disappeared and dry land was at its feet.

"Havers, Mr. Freeth. It looks as if it's seeking to
cross."

"Perhaps it wants to follow us to the island."

"Nay. It's seeking to cross."

As if to remove all doubt, they heard a querulous
whine—a short series of lifting cries such as a dog
makes when it finds itself barred by something that sur-
passes its understanding.

"Aye, it's wishful to cross," the Scot repeated. "I think I'll tak' a row across by there and . . ."

As he spoke, he walked to the beach and lifted the bow of the rowboat. The shipped oars thumped in the rowlocks, and the noise went eddying across the still surface of the loch. At that moment Leslie Freeth saw the dog lift its head and then turn away.

"It's going, Mr. McBane," he called.

The Scot looked up. He straightened. The two men watched the collie turn into the underbrush. Only once in a while could they see a glimpse of the dog as it trotted steadily along the edge of the loch toward the west. It went confidently, as if now it had made up its mind.

"It's on its way the noo," McBane said. "Puir thing—it's got a long road to gang."

"You mean, it's going to walk round this loch? Why, that'd be miles and miles . . ."

"It'll ha' to gang near a hundred miles afore it can get by."

The artist stared at the older man, a little incredulously.

"You mean to tell me that a dog is going to walk a hundred miles just to get round a lake. Why . . ."

Freeth began to laugh, but McBane's tone halted him.

"Mr. Freeth, a collie is by origin a Scottish dog. And it has in it the courage and perrtinacity o' this land."

McBane said it reprovingly, and Freeth recognized the tone behind the words. His mind moved on.

"Mr. McBane."

"Aye?"

"What do you think it wants to cross for? Why should it?"

The Scotsman stood still for a long time. Then he said: "Now who could say? Only one thing, forebye.

It's got business somewheer, and it's ganging aboot its
business wi'oot asking help fra' no ither body on the
face o' this airrth. And . . ."

Here McBane turned to his boat and clambered in.
Then he continued: ". . . it's an example which all the
rest of us micht do weel to follow."

Freeth smiled to himself. The dour old man had a
habit of turning all things in nature to a stern lesson on
human conduct. His mind went back to his painting,
and his eye only half saw the boat, growing smaller
and smaller, as McBane pulled it across the water,
leaving him in solitude.

Instinct is like the flight of a bird, for its directions
are in mighty, straight lines.

So Lassie, in her quest to get home, had worked almost in a beeline toward the village of Greenall Bridge,
far to the south. Sometimes turning or bending her
path where the obstacles of towns or impassable mountains lay before her, she had always come back to the
instinctive line to the south. So she had come down
through the Highlands, day after day of endless, weary
travel. Her line had been straight.

But she had no way to foresee the land before her.
She could not know that the instinctive straight line
toward home would bring her to an impasse against the
great lochs of Scotland.

One can look at a map and see what an obstacle
these are, for they are great, long bodies of water, running almost due east and west, that almost cut the
country in two. And although they look like narrow
fingers on the map, they are not truly narrow in actual-
ity. Wide, expansive bodies of water they are, and their
far reaches are not to be swum by an animal. For narrow as they may be, the farther shoreline is often lost,
or at best a thin, low-lying stripe of faint blue.

No, the lochs are a fearful barrier. Man can cross in his boat, and ferries, but not an animal.

Yet, at the shore of the great loch, Lassie did not surrender her purpose. Her instinct told her to go south. But if the way was barred, she would seek some other way. So she started on her long trip to circle the lake. Day after day she worked west, fighting her way along, circling hamlets and villages, but always returning afterward to the lake's edge, and working west.

Sometimes it would seem as if the barrier were circled and the way free. For a spell Lassie would trot at her unfaltering pace in the desired southern direction.

But it was always just a headland that jutted out, a headland that reached into the water. And always Lassie would work to the southernmost tip and wade into the water, and with her head turned to the south would give a short, questing whine. Then always she must turn north again, back along the shore, to press west once more in her search for a way around.

Dozens of bays and headlands and just as many disappointments! A week after Leslie Freeth and McBane had seen the dog, she was still working her way west. And still the great, long loch stretched as a barrier that a dog could not understand.

When a Dog Is Ailing

Lassie trotted from a thicket and came to the shore. She was moving more slowly now, for the pads of her feet were bruised and sore, and in the delicate membrane between those pads on the right forefoot a thorn was festering. Nor was her head as high now, and there was less confidence in her way of going.

Often, at times, it seemed as if she had forgotten why she was on her endless journey. But this was never for long, and now her pace became steady again, and she quickened it, carrying herself so that her afflicted paw took less weight. Her head turned hopefully, for on her left now, at last, was no great impassable body of water. The loch had narrowed to a river. But it was a tumultuous, fast-charging river that cascaded fiercely over the rocky bed.

Lassie came to the water's edge. She turned her head to the west again. But there, not far below her, was a town. From a bridge there were boys—fishing, shouting, filling the air with their cries. Lassie was still wary of human beings. She gazed steadily at them.

Then she looked again at the white, tumbling water. The roar of it drummed unpleasantly in her ears. Yet she hesitated only a moment. Then, boldly springing, she launched her body far out into the water.

The current caught her as a piece of paper thrown from a moving train is snatched away by the wind; and

as she landed the water bore Lassie's body downstream. The power of the river tumbled her about, but
she came to the surface and began striking out for the
far shore. Her head was outstretched, her four feet
drove steadily, pumping her along.

Again and again the current tumbled her with crushing force, and often she was submerged in swift eddies.
But each time the marvelous direction sense of a dog
never deserted her, and as she came up she was still
fighting in the right direction. A man battered on a
football field might start to carry the ball in the wrong
direction, but the direction sense of an animal is not so
easily defeated. Always Lassie struck out toward the
southern bank.

But the stream had now carried her down toward
the village. The boys on the bridge saw the spectacle of
a dog being whirled by the current. They shouted and
hallooed. With the cruelty of the young that sometimes
gets free rein, they picked stones from the roadbed and
flung them at her. As her body was whirled under the
bridge, they ran across to the downstream side and
continued their senseless pelting.

Lassie still fought on. Now she was at last nearing
the other bank. A cascade was below her. Her driving
feet raced, but they were not powerful enough. The
current caught her, and she felt herself being whirled
through space. Her body was driven cruelly against a
rock, and the stab of pain ran like fire along her side.
The current drew her down, and she disappeared.

The boys on the bridge, looking now far downstream, gave a shout, almost of insane triumph, such as
the Tuscan army might have given before the moment
of silence when Horatius leaped into the Tiber. Then
they were still. They stood gazing at the tumbling
water. At last, after it seemed that too much time had
passed, they shouted again. There, in a backwater,

Lassie's head broke the surface, and she was still driving with her legs. Now the water was still, and she was able to master it. Fighting, swimming, driving with all her force, she made the landing. Her feet touched ground. The water soaked into her coat seemed to be too much of a burden, for she staggered at that moment, and her weary muscles seemed unable to hold her.

She started to drag herself clear. But now, for the first time, she became aware of another danger. The troop of boys was dashing down the riverbank, sounding a wild chorus. Lassie called on her last strength. She pulled herself up the bank. She did not even wait to shake the water from her coat. She did not halt for the old pain in her forefoot nor for the new one that seared like fire along her side. Her mind held only one thing.

At last she was across. After weary days of thwarted direction sense, she was at last free—free to go south. The barrier was passed.

She broke into a clumsy lope. The noise of the lads behind her faded.

Now that the great barrier of the loch was circled at last, Lassie drove in her desired direction with clearer intensity. The village and the shouting boys were soon left behind. She dropped from the gallop to the slow trot that covered the most ground with the least effort.

The pain in her side and in her forepaw did not come into her mind. She adjusted her gait as best she could to favor the injuries.

Soon she left the road behind and set her path across meadows and flatlands. At sundown she was still traveling, as if, now that she could follow the line south again after so many days of going westward, she could not travel long enough to satisfy the urge within her. It was long past nightfall when at last she denned up where a clump of gorse arched over beside a field-wall.

She lay close to the ground. The coolness of the earth there, sheltered from all suns, felt good to the burning ache in her side. She licked at the forepaw, trying with her tongue to reach between the pads where the thorn festered. For · nearly an hour she worked, but in the end the thorn still rested there.

With a sigh that was almost like that of a tired man, she crossed her muzzle over her extended foreleg and closed her eyes.

It was not yet dawn when she woke. She yawned and tried to raise herself. Her forequarters came from the ground. But her hindquarters did not move. She sat for a moment as if in surprise at this new and puzzling problem. Then again she strained, pulling with the muscles of her shoulders. For a second she managed to stand upright. She took one step forward and gave one hop with her good back leg. The other one did not work.

During the night the injury to her side had stiffened. In the last crash against the rocks in the tumbling river, she had broken one rib and bruised badly the muscles and joints of her hind leg. They had now stiffened almost to immobility.

Hobbling badly, Lassie turned round in the shelter under the gorse. Then she let herself fall heavily to the ground. She curled herself up and lay silently, her eyes staring through the mass of stalks and tendrils toward the field where the first hint of dawn was showing. She could travel no farther. Instinct told her that. She must stay there.

When human beings are ill, they often make a show of their injuries and parade them so that others may see and give them sympathy. It is just the reverse with an animal living in its natural state. Asking no sympathy, deeming rather that weakness of any kind is some-

thing to be ashamed of, it crawls away into some
hidden corner and there, alone, it awaits the outcome
—either recovery or death.

This same force held Lassie to the den beneath the
gorse. The desire to travel often wracked her, but the
animal law to stay hidden during injury overcame it.

For days she lay, coiled and hidden away, her eyes
bright but unmoving. Outside, the world went through
its cycles. The darkness and the daylight followed each
other. The birds sang. Once some field laborers passed.
Sometimes the wind brought the unmistakable hot,
near scent of a rabbit. Once a weasel, questing through
the field, came part way through the gorse toward the
den. His sharp eyes saw the coiled, furry shape. His
nose trembled. For a moment he stood, unmoving;
then he turned calmly and went on his way as if knowing the sick animal had no desire to pursue him.

All those things passed, but Lassie did not stir. The
fever raged in her and possessed her body.

For six days she lay, almost without a move. Then,
on an afternoon, as the sun was slanting lower, she
lifted her head at last. Slowly, weakly, she began to lick
her forepaw. Nature had done its work. From the festering sore the thorn had worked its way. Little by little, Lassie licked it clear and then cleaned the wound.
She looked about her. Slowly she struggled to her feet.
Her bad hind leg hung, not touching the ground.
Slowly she limped from her hiding place. Hobbling
across the field, she went downhill to where her nose
told her there was water. She found the tiny streamlet,
lowered her head, and lapped. It was the first time she
had drunk for a week.

Greedily she took the water. She lay down by the
stream but her head now stayed erect. Her nose lifted,
and she gave the sharp, protesting cry. She stood and

faced to the south. Then she looked back to the gorse
clump. At last she turned and hobbled again up the
hill.

Now some of the stiffness was gone from her body
and she managed to go quite freely on three legs. Returning to the gorse clump, she crawled into the shelter
and lay there, patiently, waiting for the night.

For two more days she rested there, making brief
trips to the stream to quench her thirst. But of food,
she had none, nor did she seem to desire any.

Nine days after she had crossed the turbulent river,
she came out from her den and made her way to the
drinking place. Now she looked as if she were using all
four feet, but the bad hind leg was carrying no
weight—only going stiffly through an imitation of its
function.

She lapped the clear water and, as before, raised her
head afterward and looked toward the south. In her
mind something was stirring. It was the time sense.

Faintly in the depth of her mind the time sense,
which had been blotted out during her illness, woke
again.

It was time—time to go—time to go for . . .

Then Lassie knew once more. This was the time she
should be keeping the rendezvous at the schoolhouse.
But the school—it was there—in that direction. That
was the way to go!

She turned her head once and looked back up the
field toward the gorse clump by the wall. But it was
only for a moment. Then, stiffly, she crossed the
stream. Going slowly, she struck out to the south. Lassie was on her way again.

This was no proud show collie that trotted boldly. It
was a travel-stained dog, its body weak and pinched,
wracked from the long days of starvation and with the

fever that had passed. It was a painful shuffle rather than a proud trot that carried the dog along. And it did not last long.

Shortly after sundown Lassie halted again, this time by a snug walled-in place. It was a shoot-point in which the wealthy men stood hidden as the birds were driven over them during the grouse season; but Lassie did not know this. All she knew was that it gave her protection and warmth.

Nor did Lassie know that she had come but three miles from the den under the gorse clump. The greatness, or the smallness, of a distance do not qualify in the minds of an animal. All she knew was that she felt satisfied. She had made her way in the direction in which she wanted to go more than she wanted anything else in life. She breathed happily.

She lifted her ears, and the tip of her nose moved. The scent of rabbit came to her clearly. .

Food! At last she was aware of it again and desired it. A ravening hunger woke in her, and the saliva formed in her mouth. She edged herself forward from the corner of the shooting-point. Soon she would eat again. And soon she would travel again, with recovered strength.

She edged forward silently.

If she was too weak and slow now to capture food for herself, she must die. For she would soon be weaker from starvation. If she was strong enough and quick enough now to capture food, soon she would be stronger.

She crept forward, going like a ghost toward her quarry.

For to Kill the Beasties

Two men crouched in a rude, stone hut. The moonlight coming through the gap in the wall above them revealed them faintly. They were dressed alike, in rough homespun tweed, except that the younger one wore a peaked cap and the other a great woolen tam-o'-shanter. For a long time there was nothing but the sound of their breathing. Then the younger one stirred.

At that moment the older put out his hand to quiet him.

"Whist," he said.

They froze into stillness.

"Did ye hear aught, Andrew?" the younger whispered.

"I thocht. . . ."

Silently they rose and stared out through the rectangular gap in the wall. Stretching away below them was the moonlit land, the grassy fields looking like those of a well-ordered park in the faint smoky-blue of a thin mist.

They stared a long time, their eyes and ears alert.

"Nay, Andrew, I don't hear a thing."

The older man nodded, so that the tuft on his tam-o'-shanter bobbed back and forth.

"I just thocht I did."

With the tension lifted, the younger man absent-mindedly took his pipe from his pocket. The other regarded him disapprovingly.

"I wadn't smoke, Jock. Och, they'd smell it clear."

"Aye—that's so. But I'm dying for a smoke. And they'd smell them first, wouldn't they?"

Jock nodded his head toward a great pen in the field below. There, in the moonlight, the great flock of sheep stood unmoving and still. They were packed so close together that their backs made a sea of gray.

"And they'd here aught long afore us," Jock continued, motioning with his head back over his shoulder. "At least, ma Donnie would."

Hearing his name ,one of the two dogs in the shelter lifted his head expectantly. The other sighed and watched alertly to see if the long vigil was at last over.

"I don't see the idea o' keeping them in here, anyhow, Andrew. We should leave 'em ootside by the sheep."

"Na, na, Jock. If they're ootside, them devils'll never come. They're that canny, lad, it passes understanding."

"Aye, they maun be canny all richt," the younger agreed. "Six nichts we sit up on guard, and not a sign of 'em. The seventh we gang to our homes for sleep, and no sooner are our ee's closed, nor doon they come on us, ravening and slaughtering. Seven lambs and two ewes! Seven lambs, mind you! Why do they no come one o' the nichts we were ready for 'em?"

The older man ignored the last question.

"Ye should be thankful, Jock. Sixteen it was Archie Forsythe lost the Sabbath. And McKenzie thirteen the nicht afore."

"Ah, the brutes. The Sabbath and all ither days is the same to them devils. The black-hairted creatures o' Satan! If I ever caught one on 'em . . ."

The younger man left the rest unsaid.

"What makes 'em do it, Andrew?"

"Ah, lad, that's one o' those things pairhaps it's not given us to onderstand. But I suppose dogs is like humans, Jock. Most on 'em is honest and trusty. But every so often there's one born that has greed and cruelty and dishonor in his heart, and while he poses daytimes as a pairfect Galahad, as soon as dark hides him he becomes what he is—a ravening devil."

"Aye, Andrew. Ye knaw, Heaven above knaws I hae a love for dogs. Why, yon beastie o' mine, there's not a thing I wadn't do for him, or a care I wadn't gie him—or a trust I wadn't put in him. But they devils o' sheepkillers—they're not dogs. Ye knaw, Andrew, what I think sometimes?"

"What, Jock?"

"Weel, ye may laugh. But times I think them sheepkillers is not dogs, but they're the ghosts o' murderers who've been hanged that return disguised i' the body o' animals!"

The young man said that in such an eerie tone that they both shuddered. Then the older shook off the feeling.

"Na, na, Jock. They're just dogs—and ravening ones that's gone bad. And we should hae no pity on 'em."

"Ah, I'll hae no pity—if I ever see one. If I draw a bead on one o' em . . ."

"Whist!"

They froze again as the older man gave his signal.

"There it is!"

"Where?"

"Just dipped over the rise, Jock! Get yer gun, man. Quick!"

The younger grasped his rifle that leaned against the wall, and they waited. The silence grew too long.

"Ah, ye're seeing things, Andrew," the younger said finally, "there's naught. Nor will be, while we're here. The devils, they knaw we're waiting. They knaw it!"

"Hush, Jock. Be still, will ye?"

The younger complied. But the long minutes dragged, and the tedium was too much for him. He spoke again.

"Andrew."

"Aye?"

"Ye knaw, I were just thinking. It's curious that wi' us, a dog should be our greatest helper and also our greatest enemy."

"That's it, Jock. It's because they're so clever to help us, they become so clever to hurt us when they turn bad. And any of 'em can turn bad, too, Jock. Don't forget that. Even your ain beastie that ye treasure so much. Once they taste sheep blood, they become killers."

"Not ma Donnie!"

"Nay, nor I think ma Vic, either. But it's true. Once ony of 'em kill, they're started, and they go on killing not for food, but for the joy o' bloody slaughtering."

"Ma Donnie wadn't!"

"Ye can never tell, Jock. There's some dogs, now, that'll be pairfect and upricht wi' their ain flock. Then, comes nicht, they'll travel far awa'—sometimes meeting like by appointment wi' ithers o' their kind. Then like a pack o' wolves they'll descend ravening on the flock, and they'll tear through 'em, killing and slaughtering, and they'll be awa' again afore help comes. Then they'll separate, and each steal back hame. And come the next day, they'll guard their ain flock as if butter wadn't melt i' their mouths."

"Ah, but not ma Donnie. If I thocht he did . . ."

They were silent a while. Then Jock spoke again.

"It seems sad that us wha hae the greatest fondness for dogs must destroy 'em."

"Aye—but little destroying we'll do if we keep chattering all nicht. They'd never come."

The silence settled again, and the patch of moonlight moved across the floor of the rude croft. And then, at last, the older man spoke again, this time his voice trembling with emotion.

"Here they come!"

The other jumped to position, leaning his rifle on the ledge. They both stared, breath-held, at the landscape far to their left.

"Aye, there!"

Jock sighted along his rifle. There was a movement by the stone wall. Then, beyond the lined sights of the gun he saw a dog. There was no air of stealth to it. It came over the wall and trotted plainly into view.

It was Lassie. It was a week since she had left her den, but she still traveled with a limp. She came over the field in the clear moonlight, going straight and steady as if following a compass route.

In the stone hut the older man released his pent breath.

"Let him have it, Jock," he cried, in a hoarse whisper.

The younger man cuddled his rifle, but did not fire.

"Where's the others?"

"What's the odds? Let him have it."

"It's a collie—d'ye ken wha's it is?"

"Nay. It's a stray—one o' them wild ones, forebye. Let it have it, lad. Don't miss, now."

Jock turned his head.

"I handled one o' these things in the war, Andrew. I dinna miss—not when I pay for ma own ammunition."

"Then let fly, Jock!"

The younger man cuddled the stock of his rifle again. He held his breath. Slowly he brought the sights in line—now he saw over the vee of the hindsight the steady, unwavering tip of the foresight. Above it was the tiny figure of a trotting collie. The collie moved, but it always stayed in the tip of the foresight as the gun followed it along.

Jock took up the slack on the trigger. He felt the "second pull" beginning to take up.

"Hurry, Jock, now!"

Jock lifted his head and laid the rifle down.

"I canna do it, Andrew."

"Shoot it, man, shoot it!"

"Na, na, Andrew. It doesna look like one o' them devils. Look, it pays no heed to aught. Let's see if it gangs near the sheep. For it seems to be paying no heed to them at all. Look."

"It's a stray. We have a richt to shoot it!"

"Let's see if it gangs near the sheep. If it does . . ."

"Och, ye gormless! Shoot it!"

The older man's voice rose in urgent tones. The cry floated over the night to where Lassie trotted. She paused in her tracks and turned her head. Then it all struck her together—the sound of men, the scent of them, the movement in the window of the stone hut. It was man—man that would chain her, man that she must avoid.

She wheeled and sprang away in a sudden lope.

"There! It's seen us! Let him have it!"

The sudden dash of Lassie half convinced the younger man that he had misjudged the dog below. For Lassie's actions were like those of a guilty dog.

He lifted the rifle quickly, cuddled the stock, and fired.

At the crack that shattered the night, Lassie leaped away. The ugly whine of a bullet passing by her left shoulder made her veer quickly to the right. She raced across the field. There was another shot, and she felt a burning shock in her flank.

"Nay, I hit it."

"Ye didna. Look at it go!"

Inside the small shelter the voices of the men mixed with the noise of the dogs, who now cried pandemonium. "Let 'em out!"

The old man raced to the door and opened it. The dogs, then the men, tumbled out, and raced away after Lassie's tracks.

"Go get it! Sic 'em!" yelled Andrew.

The dogs raced along, baying at the chase. They went down the slope, bellies flat and their bodies almost doubling in two with the urgency of their speed. Following them came the men, but they were soon left behind. The dogs suddenly swerved, and bayed louder—for they had picked up the trail—the warm scent of new blood.

Ahead of them Lassie galloped. Twice she halted suddenly and snapped at the flank where the bullet had creased her leg muscles. She could hear the pursuing dogs behind, but she did not increase her pace. She had no fear of dogs. It was man she wished to leave behind, and her senses told her they were not near. But now she feared him more than ever. Not only could his hands chain and pen one up, but he could make the terrifying thunder noises that hurt the ears and that somehow reached out like a long, invisible whip and brought pain such as that which now tore at her.

Truly man was an evil menace.

Steadily she loped along, feeling that perhaps she would soon leave them all behind.

But the other dogs were fresh. They had not traveled, half-starved, for hundreds of weary miles. And they were soon within sight of her. They bayed a higher note and, despite the best speed that Lassie could attain, they caught up with her. Then one charged at her flank, tearing it with his teeth and buffeting her with his shoulder to bring her down.

But one thing Lassie still had. She might be weary

and starved. But she had no cowardice. She whirled like lightening and stood, fearless. Her mane stood erect, and her lips were drawn back from her fangs.

Her attitude halted the other dogs in their tracks, for though of a much rougher breed, they were of collie blood, too. And they understood the warning.

Here was no cur to be chivvied and chased like a rabbit.

As if she had driven away a petty worry, Lassie turned in obedience to that great driving force inside her. She must go on her way—south and ever south.

But the others took it for a signal of fear, and together they charged. They tore past her, as collies will, slashing as they went. For collies do not rush and hold. Their way of fighting is not like that of the bulldog; nor like that of the terrier, which dodges and worries and shakes. They rather desire to run past an enemy, giving the long, slashing wounds that wear a foe down.

It was Lassie's own way of fighting, and instinctively she knew how to meet it. However, as she whirled to meet one adversary, the other would race in and slash from the other direction. But Lassie pivoted, waiting to meet the nearest foe. She stood, her head erect, watchful in the moonlight. The one behind her charged. She dodged it and started on her way again. But the other was racing in. She turned again—a second too late. The charge buffeted her and she half fell. The other raced in before she could regain her feet. The three became a snarling, composite pile. Lassie fought herself free. And then it began all over again—one dog charging, the other racing in as she turned to meet the first.

The battle was long, and it was still going on as the men arrived, panting from their long run. They stood and watched.

"Dinna ye shoot the noo, Jock," Andrew puffed. "Ye micht hit ma Vickie."

Jock nodded, and cradled the gun on his arm. His head was thrust forward. He watched closely the battle that the one, tired, travel-weary dog put up against the two sturdy ones, rough and heavy and hard from their years of work. And often he thought that the two must win.

But Lassie had something that the others had not. She had blood. She was a pure-bred dog, and behind her were long generations of the proudest and best of her kind.

This theory of blood lines in animals is not an empty one, as any animal lover knows. Where the cold-blood horse will quit and give no more, the thoroughbred will answer and give another burst of speed gallantly, even if he is spending the last ounce of life strength; where the mongrel dog will whine and slink away, the pure-bred will still stand with uncomplaining fearlessness.

And it was this blood that won for Lassie. As one dog charged, she met him. Unmindful of the other coming at her flank, she drove him down. He lay in a moment of surrender.

Then Lassie did a curious thing. Instead of taking an easy victory and driving at his throat, she merely placed a forepaw stiffly over his body as if holding him there as a wrestler would. As long as he remained motionless, he would not suffer.

Then, as he lay still and unprotesting, Lassie faced the other dog. She lifted her head where the fangs gleamed white, and from her chest came the slow, low rumble of challenge.

The other dog looked at her, and then he, too, lay down and began licking a wound on his paw. It was armistice.

So the dogs stood for a moment—the one prone under Lassie's stiff paw, the other cleaning himself with an air that seemed to say: "I didn't have anything to do with this whole affair at all!"

It was only for a moment that picture remained, and then the madness of the fight left Lassie. The growl died in her throat, and she remembered what she had to do. She turned calmly and trotted away.

Only then did one of the men behind dance and lift his voice. "Now—now Jock! Shoot it!"

But the younger man did not move. For, in his mind, he was not seeing dogs, but men. He was remembering a certain day. And as he stood, the tired collie passed out of sight.

"Losh, Jock, and why did ye not shoot?"

"I could 'na, Andrew."

"And why not?"

"I were thinking o' March—March i' 1918, Andrew, when they come over us—and the regiment stood. It were like that, Andrew, yon collie. She fought the same way the Black Watch did, Andrew. I' March, back i' 1918 . . ."

"Are ye daft?"

"Nay, Andrew."

The younger man wrinkled his brow.

"March, 1918," the older man scoffed.

"Weel, it were a brave dog, anyhow, Andrew. And—and it were going somewheer—and—and—besides. I could 'na shoot, for I forgot to load up again."

"Och, now that's something. Forgot to load. I should think a sojer would never forget to load up again after he's fired."

"Weel—we ha' so many things to remember, Andrew," the younger man said.

Then, as they turned away, he clicked open the breech gently, took out the cartridge from the chamber of his rifle, and slipped it in his pocket silently. With the dogs following them, the men went back to the rude shelter on the moonlit slope.

A Captive in the Lowlands

The country had changed now. There were no more
Highlands and heather, no more rolling hills and sheep
pastures. Instead the country was flatter, and the only
eminences were the "bings" or slag-tips where the
waste from the coal mines was piled by the great industrial conveyers.

There were many more towns here and many more
roads. And no longer could a dog pass unobserved
around the towns, nor could it keep out of sight of
men, for there were men everywhere. No matter how
Lassie might try to circumvent them, she must come
within sight of them to make her way south.

So she developed a new attitude toward them. She
kept as far away as possible, but if she had to pass
close to them, she ignored them.

Actually, she felt much easier about the men of this
country, for in many ways they were like the men
among whom she had grown up. Their faces were often black with grime, as they had been in Greenall
Bridge. Their clothes were coated with muck, and in
the men's hands or on their heads were lanterns. And
more than that, the men and the towns carried about
them the scent of human beings who work under-
ground. This scent was much like that that Lassie's
master had worn—but these men were not her master.
They were like the others in the village, though.

And so Lassie, although now much warier, treated
these men as she had treated those other men in her
own village: she accepted them, but responded to none
of them, nor went where they could touch her, nor
answered any of their commands. For they did command her. In the industrial lowlands of Scotland there
are, as in Yorkshire, many who are knowing about
dogs. They can spot good ones and tell with a glance
when a dog is a stray. And so often these men would
say: "Look, Archie! A stray! And a good 'un, too. Hi,
here, lass! Come here then, come, lass!"

They would stretch out their hands and snap their
fingers and call in kindly tones. But although Lassie often heard in their commands a sound that was almost
like the speaking of her own name, she never responded. If the outstretched hands came too near, she
faded away from under the touch like quicksilver. If
they pursued, she would make her weary, battered
body break from the trot and drive into a lope that
would soon put her beyond the reach of two-footed
pursuers.

Once clear, she would go back to her trot, heading
south.

That trot was slower now, for there was another
thing about the changing land. There was no food.
Once there had been rabbits, but these had become
scarcer and scarcer until now it was seldom that her
nose caught the warm smell. Lassie felt the impulse to
make her muscles drive her along at any speed becoming harder and harder to command. She even felt it
harder to obey the impulse to keep away from man.
Her greater fatigue made her too weary to worry about
him unless his hand was very near.

But one impulse did not die—to keep on going
south. Never any other direction but south. So, slowly,
Lassie came down through the Lowlands of Scotland.

Her trail went through that black industrial country as she obeyed the unquenchable flame that burned in her—the desire to go south—always south. And behind her on that trail she left many stories—words that flowed in homes and cottages.

A young wife at the table in a home in a small mining town, watching her husband eat his evening meal, said:

"I had the oddest thing today, Ivor—with a dog."

"A dog? Whose?"

"I don't know who it belonged to. I was sitting outside with the baby, getting a few minutes of sun, when this dog came down the road. It was aye so muddy and forlorn and terrible-looking, but nice-looking in a way . . ."

"How could it be nice-looking and terrible-looking?"

"I don't know, now. But it was. And it looked so tired. It just looked like the men on the shift sometimes when they're coming off—so tired and weary, and yet—keeping going. So I called it, but it wadn't come. It just stood off away and looked at me—and little Ivor. So I went in and got a dish o' water and put it doon. And it came over and lapped that up. So then I got a bowl o' scraps and put them doon. And it looked a long time and walked round one way and then another, and finally came over and smelled and then began to eat—very dainty it was, but I could swear it was half starved. It was that poor and thin.

"Then, right in the middle, as it was eating, it stopped and lifted its head and started off right down the road just as if it had remembered an appointment . . ."

"Weel what did ye want it to do? Stop and say thank you?"

"No, but to richt off in the middle o' eating! Now why should it do that?"

"Ah, Peggy, and how should I know? All I do know is that ye'd be feeding all the stray dogs and waifs and tramps in the world if ye had your way."

Then the man laughed, and the woman laughed, too, for by the warmth of her husband's voice she knew that he was pleased with her.

And so she forgot the stray dog to which she had shown kindness.

In a town fifty miles to the south a thin-faced woman wrote a letter to her husband who was away on a business trip. The letter read:

"We had a frightful experience the other day. We had a mad dog in the village. Constable Macgregor saw it first and suspected it, for it had saliva flecked on its mouth. He tried to catch it, but it eluded him. I saw it coming down the street—I had been visiting Mrs. Tamson—and a terrible creature it was, with its mouth gaping open, and galloping wildly. The constable and many of the town boys were after it. I ran into Jamison's drapery and didn't come out for nearly an hour, it gave my heart such a turn.

"I heard later that they cornered it down Fennel's Alley, and they thought they had it, but at the last moment it jumped over the rear wall, which, as you know, is at least six feet high. So it must have been mad, for no sane animal would have thought of attempting such a thing.

"Since then we have had a rabies scare, and all stray dogs are being rounded up and taken to the pound. I think they should shoot all stray dogs, for one never knows what damage they may cause.

"I tell you, I have been very nervous about the whole thing, so I hope you hurry back as soon as you can possibly end your trip . . ."

Stories of cowardice and fear—as well as of trust and love—lay in the long trail over which Lassie patiently fought her way toward home.

By the great Scottish industrial city the river is broad. Along its banks are high walls and fences, for space on the river frontage is valuable—almost the lifeblood of the community.

There, by the river, the towering cranes pick up gigantic pieces of metal. They move them to the frameworks where skeletons of steel arise. There the men clamber all day, drilling and riveting, adding the harsh tattoo to the mighty thumping of steam hammers. And there the great ships that later race across the Atlantic are born.

The shipyards and the city are sprawled over every inch of the wide river. To cross from side to side there are the chugging ferries—and in the city the aged bridges that have carried traffic north and south for centuries.

And over one of those busy bridges Lassie trotted. For days she had roamed the northern bank, seeking some way to cross, but this at last was her solution— she must walk among men.

As she went along, often persons on the crowded pavement turned their heads and spoke a word to her, but she paid no attention and threaded her way along, and was soon lost to view in the crowds.

But there were two men who did not let her get out of sight. They were on a truck, crossing the bridge. One, on the front seat, merely nudged his companion who drove, and pointed toward the dog that went so intently. The other did not answer. But he nodded as if in happy agreement and set his truck at a speed that allowed them to keep Lassie in sight.

At the end of the bridge, Lassie stepped forward steadily. Her trot quickened a trifle, for now she felt at peace with her desire to get south. The river was behind her. For a second a flash of vigor flowed over her, and her tail lifted a little higher so that she looked almost gay.

She went along the pavement to the south. She did not heed the truck pulling up beside her. Among the multiple dins and smells of the city, there was no chance for her keen ears or nose to give her warning. Only at the last second, her animal senses warned her, and she gave a leap. Something was moving through the air. She drove with her legs—but it was no use. About her was a net that strangled her efforts.

For a full minute she fought, slashing at the imprisoning web. But she was only held the tighter. And now, kneeling beside her, was one of the men from the truck. He was holding her with expert hands. A thong was being twisted cruelly about her muzzle, clamping her jaws shut. Another thong went about her neck. Still another was binding her legs together.

Lassie lay still. Now she was ringed in by people.

She felt the net being lifted. With a mighty wrench she tried to tear away. Her forefeet came free! One hind leg was free! She was getting away!

Lunging and wrenching, she fought against the man who held her. Now the other had thrown his body on her. If only she had the thong about her jaw free! She felt a strain as one man grabbed at her foreleg. Then she was being beaten over the head.

She lay half-stunned. And then the men halted their beating, for a voice came, very clear, from the crowd. It was a woman's voice, one with clipped accents: "Here, you don't have to treat that dog as savagely as that!"

One of the men looked up from his kneeling.

"Who's a-doin' this job?" he asked.

Someone in the crowd started to snicker, but the laugh died as the young woman stepped forward. Her voice was stern.

"And if you think being impertinent is going to help you, you're mistaken. I've watched this entire proceeding, and I intend to report you—for both impertinence and cruelty."

When the man spoke again, his tone had changed.

"Very sorry, mum; but it's my duty, it is. And ye can't be too careful. There's a lot of mad dogs around—and a dog catcher's got to do his duty. It's public protection."

"Nonsense—this dog has no signs of rabies."

"Ye can't tell, mum. Anyhow, it's a stray—and we've got to pick up all strays. It's got no name on its collar."

The young woman made as if to speak, but the man beside her touched her arm.

"Chap's right, Ethelda. Can't have hordes of homeless dogs running about. Got to have some sort of control, y'know."

"That's right, sir," the dog-catcher said.

The girl looked about her. Then her jaw set.

"Well, they don't have to control it that way. Get up, I'll put it in the van for you."

"It'll get away from ye, mum."

"Nonsense. Stand up."

"We'll only have to go through it all over again, mum."

"Stand up!"

The kneeling men looked at the crowd, as if to say what a hopeless thing it was to argue with a woman who had silly ideas. Then, as they rose, the girl kneeled. For a second Lassie felt calm hands touching her, stroking her gently, soothing her with a soft voice.

"All right. Give me a leash—and take that net away."

The men obeyed. The girl put the thong gently round Lassie's neck. With one hand patting and calming, she pulled gently at the lead with the other.

"Come—stand up," she said.

Lassie did what her years of training had taught her. She obeyed. She followed the gentle touch of the lead. She walked to the van. As the man opened the door, the girl lifted the thin collie in, and the grilled door clanged.

"There," she said severely. "You don't have to treat even stray dogs like wild beasts."

She turned and strode away, paying scarcely any attention to the man beside her.

"A fearful scene to make in public, Ethelda," he said at last.

She did not answer, and they walked on across the bridge. Midway over, he looked at her and then stopped.

"Forgive me," he said. "I should be kicked. You were very fine."

They stopped and gazed in silence down the busy river.

"I wonder why it is," he said at length, "a man always has a horror of making a show in public. Often he wants to do—well, something exactly like what you did, and he doesn't. Sort of cowardice I suppose it is. Women are braver. You were very fine—and that's what I should have said in the first place."

The young woman placed her hand on his coat sleeve in a gesture of understanding. "It isn't me. It's the dog," she said. "You know, she reminded me so much of Bonnie. You remember Bonnie, the collie we had when I was small?"

"Oh, so I do—I'd forgotten. Well, but she was a

magnificent creature, Ethelda."

"So was this one, somehow, Michael. Oh, she was starved and bony, but somehow she reminded me of Bonnie. The same sort of patience and—and—as if she understood so much that it was a crime she couldn't speak to tell about it."

The man nodded and drew out his pipe. They leaned their arms on the parapet.

"What will they do with her?" the young woman asked at last.

"Who—the blighters with the van?"

"Yes."

"Oh, take her to the pound."

"I know, but what do they do there—with stray dogs?"

"I dunno. Seems to me they keep them or something—specified length of time. Then if no one shows up they, er, do away with them."

"They'll kill her?"

"Oh, it's quite humane. Gas chamber, or something like that. Absolutely painless, they say. Just like going to sleep. Law, or something, about it."

"And no one can save her—I mean if her owner doesn't hear about it?"

"I think not."

"Isn't there a law or something—if you go to the pound, you can claim a dog? That is, if you pay the costs and what-not?"

The man puffed his pipe.

"Seems to me there is—or there should be."

He looked up at the girl beside him. Then he smiled.

"Come on," he said.

"Donnell! Never Trust a Dog!"

The van with its grilled door drew into a courtyard. The iron gates set in the great wall clanged behind it. The van backed up so that it was tight against a raised entrance.

Inside, Lassie lay quietly in a corner. There were other dogs in the van. During the ride through the city, they had lifted their voices in clamor. But Lassie had lain still, like a captive queen among lesser prisoners. She had lain there, only her eyes alert, shutting out the exterior world just as she had done when she lay ill beneath the gorse clump.

She did not drop this air of dignity even when the grilled backdrop of the van was opened. The other dogs of mixed breeds yelped anew and darted about. The two men seized them and urged them along toward a large, concrete chamber. But Lassie did not move. Then she was the only one left in the van.

Perhaps it was her calm and regal air that misled the man. Or perhaps, too, he remembered the facility with which the young woman had placed the dog in the truck.

He entered the van with a small leash. Lassie lay quietly, and as she had been too proud to struggle and yelp for freedom as the other dogs had done, now she calmly suffered the hands to slip the thong over her head. As the lead was about to tighten she rose obediently, and as she had been taught to do from youth, began to follow the man. Down they came over the tail-board of the van and into the echoing corridor, Lassie going without either pulling ahead on the leash or dragging behind on it.

This, too, may have lulled the man, for, just as they reached the place where his assistant was holding open the barred door, he leaned down to unslip the leash.

In that flash, Lassie was free.

She leaped away like the passing of a beam of light. The man jumped to bar her path, but his human coordination was snail-like compared to that of the animal. Lassie turned herself in flight even as he started to move and drove herself between his legs and the wall.

Down the corridor she went, and then she pulled to a halt. Her way was blocked. There was nothing before her but the looming interior of the van that she had just left, backed so truly against the entrance that there was not an inch of space on any side.

She turned and dashed back—straight into the faces of the men who charged after her. Dodging their arms and legs, she catapulted past them again. At the left was a stairway. She raced for it. At the top a corridor stretched crosswise. One direction went south. She raced down it.

Now, behind her, the building began to echo with cries. There were people in the corridor. Hands grabbed at her as she raced along. Twisting like a football "back," she went the length of the corridor. And then she halted. The corridor ended at a blank wall. There was a window, but it was closed.

Lassie wheeled. Now, back down the long hall men were gathered. They were advancing. Lassie looked about her. There were many doors at each side of the way, but they were all closed. There was no escape.

Her captors seemed to be confident of that, for now

the two men with peaked caps appeared, and the voice of the dog-catcher rose.

"Stay where ye are, everyone, please. We've got her now. Just stay where ye are so's she can't get back down the corridor. She won't bite anybody. She's not a bad dog."

Slowly the man advanced. Behind him was his assistant with the net. They came nearer and nearer.

Proudly Lassie stood at bay. With head high, she waited.

And then escape came. For right beside Lassie, one of the forbidding doors opened, and a voice sounded. It was an important voice—an official voice.

"What's going on out here? Do you realize there's a Court of Law sitting . . ."

That was as far as he got. For at that moment a tawny figure streaked by him, almost upsetting him as it cannoned off his legs. His face twisted itself into an expression of horror and outraged dignity. He gave one glance of utter contempt to the two men with the net. Then he shut the door.

Now, inside the room the air echoed with sound, for Lassie was racing about, looking for some means of escape. But in that large room there seemed to be none. All the doors were closed. At last, in a corner, Lassie stood at bay. People moved away from her, leaving her isolated. The banging and scraping of chairs and the cries slowly sank, and the only noise left was that of a thumping gavel. Then a sombre voice spoke. "Do I understand that this is the surprise witness that the defense has promised?"

Immediately the room rocked with laughter. Young men in sombre costumes smiled broadly. The imperious figure wearing the enormous white wig allowed himself to smile, too, for he was famed far and wide for his piercing wit. And, moreover, this case had been

long and tedious. His remark would be repeated and
reprinted in newspapers the length and breadth of the
land:

"Another report comes today concerning the spar-
kling humor of that renowned legal wit, Justice
McQuarrie, sitting at . . ."

The great man nodded affably so that his wig almost
came onto his forehead. At that moment, Lassie
barked, once, shortly. The great man beamed.

"I presume that is an answer in the affirmative. And
I may add that this is the most intelligent witness I
have had before me in twenty years, for it is the first
one that can answer yes or no without equivocation."

Again the great room rocked with laughter. The
young men in gowns nodded like mandarins and turned
to one another.

Old McQuarrie was in excellent form today!

Now, as though deciding that he alone should decree
how long laughter should last, the judge thumped with
the gavel. His brow furrowed. His eyes were stern.

"Sergeant. What is that?"

A uniformed man hastened before the tribunal and
stood at attention.

"Sergeant. What is that?"

"It is a dog, Your Lordship."

"A dog!"

The judge turned his glance on the animal, still at
bay in the corner.

"You confirm my own suspicions, Sergeant. It is a
dog!" the judge said affably. Then his voice broke into
a roar. "Well, what do I want done with it?"

"I think I know what is in your mind, Your Lordship."

"What is in my mind, Sergeant?"

"You wish it removed, Your Lordship."

"I do! Remove it! Remove it!"

The Sergeant looked about him in hurt amazement.
In all his years as an official, such a problem had never
before arisen. Perhaps it had never arisen in all the history of law. Perhaps there was no official and recognized procedure set down by any book or statute for
the proper engineering of such a matter. Every other
possible thing had been thought of, but—dogs? Not
that the Sergeant could remember.

Dogs—from court, removal of. Perhaps it was listed
somewhere. But the Sergeant couldn't remember it.
And if there were no official course of action to be followed, how should one . . .

The Sergeant's face suddenly brightened. He had
solved it. The stairway of authority. He turned toward
the man who had opened the door and allowed Lassie
to enter.

"McLosh! Remove this dog. Where did it come
from?"

The red-faced guardian of the door looked reproach-
fully at his superior.

"Na doot she's wiggled awa' fra' Fairgusson and
Donnell. They twa's oot there the noo wi' a lashin' o'
ropes."

The Sergeant turned and translated in more official
language to the judge.

"The dog's escaped from the pound authorities,
Your Lordship. Two of them are outside now. And
since the apprehension and detention of stray dogs
properly comes within the duties of the pound . . ."

"I won't make an official ruling on that, but unofficially, Sergeant—unofficially . . ."

Again the delighted young men in robes smiled at
each other.

". . . Unofficially I should say it is in their province.
Admit them and order them to remove this animal."

"Very good, Your Lordship."

Escaping hurriedly, the Sergeant went to the door.

"Get it oot o'here, quick. Before he loses his temper," he whispered huskily.

Bearing the net, the two men entered the court. The legal array stood in eager interest. It was certainly a relief from the droning on this dull day.

The two men crept toward the corner, slowly—warily.

"We'll soon ha' here out o' here, Your Lordship," one said in a conciliating tone.

But as he spoke, Lassie wheeled away. She knew that net. It was a hateful enemy. She must escape it.

Again the room became bedlam. The younger men took every advantage of the situation, and like schoolboys they lifted their voices in hunting cries.

"Yoicks! Gone away!"

"Look! Hallo, Watson. There by the desk!"

"Tallyho! Hiii! Ow, my shin."

Cheerily they whooped, and in high glee did their best in every way to impede the men with the net—managing to upset them at every opportunity as they pretended to help corner the dog.

But at last the fun had run its course. Lassie was penned by the wall. The ring of men crept nearer. Above her was an open window. She leaped to the ledge—and then stood there in hesitation, for below her was the courtyard where the van still stood. There was a sheer drop of twenty feet to the concrete below.

The men came forward confidently. They knew that it was too far to leap. They spread out the net.

On the ledge Lassie trembled. Off to the left was the roof of the van. It was only ten feet below, but it was too far away. She crouched, her paws dancing as if to get better footing. Her muscles trembled.

For a dog is not like a cat. Like men, a dog has learned to fear heights. And yet it was the only way.

Crouching, gathering her muscles, Lassie stood. Then she leaped. Out she drove, as far as she could, toward the top of the van. Even as she went through the air, she knew she was falling short. Her sense of time and balance told her she could not land safely. Reaching out with her forelegs, she just touched. For a brief second she hung there, as her hind legs scrambled on the side. Then she dropped to the ground heavily. And she lay, stunned.

Above, in the courtroom, the windows were lined with faces. The dog catcher gave a sharp cry.

"Now we've got her."

He turned with his companion, but they were stopped by a sharp command. The judge frowned at them, and when he spoke it was as if all humor had gone from the day.

"This is a Court of Law. You will go quietly. Gentlemen, please. I will declare a recess."

The gavel thumped, and all stood as the age-old cry of "Oyez!" sounded.

Grumbling, the two men made their way from the room. Once in the corridor they raced along.

"That bloomin' dog," the older panted. "I'll show 'er. Wait till I get . . ."

But when they got to the courtyard, they looked about in amazement. There was the van. There was the spot where Lassie had lain, stunned. But she was not there. The yard was empty.

"Well, if it isn't the end of a bloomin' perfect day, Donnell," the older puffed. "She should be dead down 'ere—and where is she?"

"Gone over the wall, Mr. Fairgusson!"

"Six foot—and she should be dead. That ain't no blasted dog, Donnell. It's a bloomin' vampire."

They went back into their quarters in the basement.

"Mr. Fairgusson. Isn't a vampire a thing wi' wings?"

"Exactly, Donnell. That's what I mean. An animal would need wings to get over that wall."

Donnell scratched his head. "Once," he said, "I saw one o' the cinema pictures aboot a vampire."

The older spoke sternly.

"Now, Donnell, here I am trying to set my mind on this matter—important matter, it is—and ye're raving aboot the cinema. Ye'll never make headway in the sairvice o' the municipality if ye go on like that. Now the thing is, what shall we do aboot this dog?"

Donnell pulled his lip.

"I dinna ken."

"Well, think. Now what would ye do if ye were alone?"

Donnell went into a deep study. At last his face broke like a sunbeam. "We tak' the van and go oot and aboot and look for her again!" The other shook his head as if he despaired of mankind.

"Donnell, aren't ye ever going to learn?"

"Learn? What ain't I learning the noo?"

"Knocking off time! Knocking off time!" Fergusson said with emphasis. "How many times have I told ye? When ye're a civil servant, ye keep yer working hours. If ye start to toil all hours o' the day and nicht, firrst thing ye know they'll be expecting it all the time."

"That's richt. I forgot."

"Forgot! Ye forgot. Set yer example by me, my lad. Then ye'll get somewhere."

The young one looked shamefaced.

"No," said the other. "Mak' yer head save yer feet. What we do the noo, is mak' oot a report."

He got pencil and paper. For a long time he sucked the end of the pencil.

"This is hard to do, Donnell," he said, at length. "It's a sort o' black mark on the escutcheon o' the department. For twenty-two years I've been here, and

never before in all ma service has a dog got awa'. And I
hardly know how to report this."

Donnell scratched his head. Then inspiration came.
"Well, look. Couldn't ye just forget it? Don't say aught
aboot it."

The other looked up in admiration.

"Ye micht ha' something there, Donnell. Ye're
learning at last. But one verra important thing ye forget. There's yon happenings in the Court. They'll be
noised aboot, wi'oot doot!"

"Aye," said Donnell, excitedly. "But ye can say we
copped the beggar at that. If they wish to test it, we
can say it's yon big rough beggar in there we copped
this morn. Just report one less in, and then ye'll not
have an escaped dog to put that blot on yer—er—
escunchon."

"Donnell, ye have it!"

Vigorously the older set to work. For half an hour
he wrote painfully. He had just finished when the
buzzer rang. The door opened and a policeman entered.
Behind him followed the young woman and man who
had stood by the bridge.

"This is the pound, sir," the policeman said.

The man advanced.

"I am informed," he said, "that on payment of
pound costs and proper fee, I can secure any un-
claimed dog here?"

"That's richt, sir."

"Well then I—er, this young lady, that is—wishes to
secure that collie captured this morning."

"Collie?" Fergusson echoed, thinking fast. "Collie.
No, there was no collie captured this morn, sir."

The young woman stepped forward.

"Look here, what are you trying to do now? You
know very well I was present when you captured a collie this morning, and handled it roughly, you did, too.

If you're up to any tricks about it, Captain McKeith here will have it looked into."

Fergusson scratched his head.

"Well, I'll tell you the truth—it escaped."

"It what?" the girl asked.

"It escaped, mum. Anyone here can tell ye about it. It broke loose and got up i' Justice McQuarrie's court and jumped fro' a window and got over the wall—and it's gone."

"Gone!" For a moment the girl stared. Then a look of happiness crept over her face.

"I don't know whether you're telling the truth or not," the young man said. "But to make sure I'm going to put in a written request for that dog."

He made a note in a small pocketbook and turned away. The girl went with him gladly.

"I'm sorry, Ethelda," he said, as they went up the stairs.

The young woman smiled.

"It's all right. I'm glad. Don't you see, it's free again. Free! Even if I don't have it—it's free!"

Downstairs in the subterranean office, Fergusson blustered before his assistant.

"Now I'll have to report it escaped, for the blighters undootedly will mak' a request for it and I'll have to explain why I canna gie 'em the dog."

Savagely he tore up his painfully written false report.

"All that fine work for naught. Now let that go for to teach ye a lesson, Donnell. What conclusion would ye draw fro' all this?"

"Never mak' oot a false report," Donnell replied, dutifully.

"Och, no," Fergusson said in scorn. "Ye'll never progress in the service, Donnell. The conclusion to draw is this: Never trust a dog!"

"Ye tak' that one. There she pretended to be as meek as a babe in arms as ye micht say. I trust her for just one second, and she turrns like a ball o' fire on Judgment Day. There she ought to be afraid to jump—and what does she do?"

"She jumps," Donnell replied.

"That richt. There she ought to be dead, and what is she?"

"She's alive."

"Richt again. Then she ought not to ha' been able to jump yon wall, and what does she do?"

"She jumps it."

"Richt once more. And so the moral is, Donnell, as long as ye're in this job, never trust a bloomin' dog. They ain't—well—they ain't human, dogs ain't. They just ain't human!"

Lassie Comes Over the Border

Slowly, steadily, Lassie came across a field. She was not trotting now. She was going at a painful walk. Her head was low and her tail hung lifelessly. Her thin body moved from side to side as though it took the effort of her entire frame to make her legs continue to function.

But her course was straight. She was still continuing to go south.

Across the meadow she came in her tired walk. She paid no attention to the cattle that grazed on the green about her and that lifted their heads from their feeding to regard her as she passed.

The grass grew thicker and coarser as she followed the path. The track became beaten mud. Then the mud was a puddle of water, and the puddle was the edge of a river.

She stood at the trampled place. It was where the cattle came to drink and to stand for coolness in the heat of the day. Beyond her some of them stood now, knee-deep in the slow backwater. They turned and regarded her, their jaws moving unceasingly.

Lassie whimpered slightly and lifted her head as if to catch some scent from the far bank. She rocked on her feet for a moment. Then, wading forward tentatively, she went deeper and deeper. Her feet now felt no bottom. The backwater began to carry her upstream. She began swimming, her tail swirling out behind her.

This was not a turbulent river like the one back in
the Highlands. It was not a dirty, factory-clustered one
like that now many miles back in the industrial city.
But it was broad, and its current went firmly, carrying
Lassie downstream.

Her tired legs drove with the beat, her forefeet
pumped steadily. The south bank moved past her, but
she seemed to be getting no nearer.

Weakness numbed her, and her beat grew slower.
Her outstretched head came under the water. As if this
wakened her from a sleep, she began threshing wildly.
Her head went straight up, and her forefeet sent a
splashing foam before her. She was a swimmer in
panic.

But her head cleared again, and once more she settled down to the steady drive forward.

It was a long swim—a courageous swim. And when
at last she reached the other shore, she was almost too
weak to climb the bank. At the first place, her forepaws scratched and she fell back. The bank was too
high. The backwater began carrying her upstream. Lassie tried again. She splashed and fell back again. Then
the eddy carried her, and at last her feet touched a
shelving bottom. She waded to shore.

As though the weight of the water in her coat were
an extra load that was too much for her to carry, she
staggered. Then dragging herself rather than walking,
she crawled up the bank. And there, at last, she
dropped. She could go no farther.

But she was in England! Lassie did not know that.
She was only a dog going home—not a human being
wise in the manner of maps. She could not know that
she had made her way all down through the Highlands,
the Lowlands; that the river she had crossed was the
Tweed, which divides England and Scotland.

All these things she did not know. All she knew was that, as she crawled higher on the bank, a strange thing happened. Her legs would no longer respond properly, and, as she was urging herself forward, the tired muscles rebelled at last. She sank, plunged a moment, and then fell on her side.

For a second, she whined. With her forepaws she clawed the earth, still dragging herself south. She was in rough grass now. She pulled herself along—a yard—another foot—another few inches. Then at last the muscles stopped their work.

Lassie lay on one side, her legs outstretched in "dead dog" position. Her eyes were glazed. The only movement was a spasmodic lifting and falling of the pinched flanks.

All that day Lassie lay there. The flies buzzed about her, but she did not lift her head to snap at them.

Evening came, and across the river was the sound of the herder and the lowing of the cows. The last notes of the birds came—the singing of a thrush through the lingering twilight.

Darkness came with its night sounds, the scream of an owl and the stealthy rippling of a hunting otter, the faraway bark of a farm dog, and the whispering in the trees.

Dawn came with new sounds—the splash of a leaping trout while the river was still veiled in mist. Then the rooks rose with their eternal cry of warning as a man left the door of the farm cottage over the fields. The sun came, and the shadows danced weakly on the grass as the overhead trees shimmered in the first breeze of the new day.

As the sun reached her, Lassie rose slowly. Her eyes were dull. Walking slowly, she set out—away from the river, going south.

* * *

The room was small and humble. In a chair beside a
table where the lamp glowed, Daniel Fadden sat, reading slowly from the newspaper. Nearer the coal fire on
the hearth, his wife sat in a rocking chair, knitting. She
teetered endlessly back and forth as her fingers flashed
over the wool and needles, so that the movements all
seemed related—one rock of the chair, three stitches
on the needles.

They were both old people, and it seemed that they
had been so long together in life that there was no longer any need to talk. They were contented just to be,
sure in the knowledge the other was near.

Finally the man pushed his steel-rimmed spectacles
back on his forehead and looked at the hearth.

"We'll do wi' a bit more coal on the fire," he said.

His wife nodded as she rocked, and her lips went
through the noiseless form of counting. She was "turning a heel" in her knitting and wanted to keep sure
count.

The man rose slowly. Taking the scuttle, he went to
the sink. In the cupboard beneath was the coal bin.
With a little shovel he slowly scooped some out.

"Ah, we're nearly oot," he said.

His wife looked over. Mentally both of them began
to count—the cost of more coal. How quickly they had
used the last hundred weight. Their lives were deeply
concerned with these things. Expenses ran very close.
All they had was the small pension that the Government paid for their son who had been killed in France.
Then each of them drew the old-age pension of ten
shillings a week given by the State. This was no wealth,
but they husbanded it carefully and owed no man. The
tiny cottage, far out on the highway from any town,
was a cheap place to live. In the little plot of land
about it, Fadden grew a stock of vegetables. He had a

flock of chickens, several ducks, and a goose "fattening for Christmas." This last was their largest and most lasting joke. Six years before, Fadden had traded a dozen early hen eggs for one tiny gosling. Carefully he had raised it, boasting about what a fine plump bird it would be by Christmas time.

It had become just that—marvelous and plump. And a few days before the holiday of holidays, Fadden had taken his hatchet, and he had sat indoors a long time, regarding it. Finally his wife, understanding, had looked up patiently.

"Dan," she said. "I just don't think I'd favor goose this year. If you did a chicken instead—and . . ."

"Aye, Dally," Fadden had said. "It would be a terrible waste—one big goose for just the two of us. Now a chicken would be just right . . ."

And so the goose was spared. Each year after that it was dutifully fattened for Christmas.

"This year it goes," Fadden would always announce. "Fattening a goose all year, just to strut and waddle round like he's king of everything. This year he goes."

And always the goose lived. Mrs. Fadden always knew it would. When Fadden announced belligerently that it was headed for the Yule oven, she would say dutifully, "Aye, Dan." And when he hemmed and hawed at the last minute and announced that a goose was much too big for the two of them, she would say, "Aye, Dan." Privately she often said to herself that the goose would be living long after, as she put it, the two of them were "deep under the ground and at rest."

But she would not have it otherwise. In fact, if Dan had ever gone through with his firmly announced intentions, she would have felt the world was dropping from under her.

Of course, it cost a lot to feed up a great, hungry goose, but one could save other ways. A penny here, a

penny there. One could always buy carefully and save
carefully, nursing the copper coins along.

So their life went, with dignity and great content—
but always with the thought of precious pennies, as it
was this evening, when they both reckoned up the
amount of coal and how long it had lasted.

"Ah, never mind mending the fire, Dan," she said.
"Just bed it up wi' ashes and we'll away to bed. We
stay up too late anyhow."

"Sit ye there awhile," Daniel said, for he knew Dally
dearly loved to rock and knit before the hearth for a
couple of hours in the evening. "It's early yet. I'll put
just a little on. For Heaven knows, it's chilly enough
tonight—nasty, cold, east rain."

Dally nodded. As she rocked she listened to the
wind howling at the east of the low house and the slat-
ting of the rain on the shutters.

"It'll be coming up for autumn soon, Dan."

"Aye, that it will. This is the first o' them easters.
And cold! Blow right through a man's body to his
bones. I'd hate to be out in it long."

His wife rocked steadily, and her mind wandered.
Whenever anyone talked of bad weather, she always
turned her mind back to young Dannie. In those
trenches they had had no warm hearths. The men had
lived their lives that first winter in muddy holes in the
ground—sleeping there of nights with no shelter. A
body would die, you would think. And yet, when Dannie had come home on leave, there he was all glowing
and healthy and fine. And when she'd asked him about
being careful to keep his chest warm and his throat
dry, he had laughed and held his sides—a big, booming, strong laugh.

"Eigh, after living through this winter i' France, it's
never cold that'll carry me off, Ma," he had boomed.

And it wasn't cold nor illness. Machine guns, his

Colonel had written in the letter that Dally still kept folded away beside her marriage license.

Ah, war—machine wars. Bullets took them all. The brave and the cowardly, the weak and the fine strong ones like Dannie. And it wasn't the dying that took bravery, then, for cowards could die. It was the living that took bravery—living in that mud and rain and cold and keeping the spirit strong through it all. That was the bravery. And how often she pictured it, when the winds blew and the cold rain slatted. All so long ago, but she still pictured it, knitting, purling, rocking—knitting, purling, rocking.

She halted her chair and sat with head erect. For a moment she was still. Then she began again—knitting, purling, rocking, thinking . . .

Again she stopped. She held her breath to hear better—hear above the sound of the fire. There was the hiss of the coal, the spit of ashes dropping in the pit beneath the grate, the crinkle of the newspaper; farther away the tap of a shutter looser than the rest, the surging smacking of rain. Farther beyond that there was another noise, out in the sweep of the wind. Or was it imagination, from thinking of Dannie so long ago?

She dropped her head. Then she sat up again.

"Dan! There's something by the chickens!"

He sat erect a moment.

"Ah now, Dallie. Ye're allus imagining things," he reproved. "There's not a thing but the wind. And that shutter's a bit loose. I'll have to fix it."

He went back to his reading, but the little gray-haired woman sat with head erect. Then she spoke again.

"There—again! There is something!"

She rose. "If you won't go see what's after your chickens, Daniel Fadden, I will!"

She took her shawl, but her husband rose.

"Now, now, now," he grumbled. "Sit ye down. If ye want me to go, I'll go just to make your soul content. Now I'll look around.'

"Wrap your muffler round your neck first, then," she reproved.

She watched him go, then she was alone in the house. Her ears, attuned by the lonesomeness to the sounds of living, heard his footsteps go away—and a few moments later, above the noise of the storm, come back quickly. He was running. She jumped up and faced the door before it opened.

"Get your shawl and come," he said. "I've found it. Where's the lantern?"

Together they hurried out into the night, leaning against the gusts of wind and rain. Going up the road, beside the hawthorn hedge that bordered the highway, at last the old man paused and scrambled down the bank. His wife held up the lantern. There she saw what her husband had found—a dog, lying in the ditch. She watched its head turn, and for a second the light glowed incandescent in its eyes as the lamp shone.

"Poor, poor thing," she said. "And who would leave their dog out a night like this?"

The words were torn away by the wind, but the old man heard the sound of her voice.

"It's too done up to walk," he shouted. "Hold the lantern up!"

"Shall I gie ye a hand?"

"Hey?"

She bent down and shouted.

"Shall I gie ye a hand?"

"No! I can manage!"

She saw him bend and pick up the animal. Grasping the shawl against the gale that would pluck it away, she went beside him, holding the lantern high.

"Go easy, Dan, now," she said. "Oh, poor, poor thing!"

She ran ahead of him to open the door. Panting, the old man struggled in. The door slammed. The two old people brought Lassie into the warmth of the hearth and laid her on the rug. They stood back a moment, looking at her. Lassie lay with eyes closed.

"I doubt it'll live till the morn," the man said.

"Well, that's no reason to stand there. We can at least try. Get your wet things off, quick, Dan, or I'll have you down, too. Look at it shiver—it isn't dead. Get that sack fro' the bottom o' the cupboard, Dan, and dry it off some."

Awkwardly the old man bent, rubbing the dog's drenched coat.

"She's awful mucky, Dally," he said. "Your nice clean hearth rug'll be all muddied up."

"Then there'll be a job for you shaking it out in the morning," she answered tartly. "I wonder if we could feed it?"

The old man looked up. His wife was holding in her hand the can of condensed milk. Their unspoken thoughts went back and forth like a silent conversation. It was the last of their milk.

"Well, we'll have tea for breakfast wi'out any," the woman said.

"Save a bit, Dally. Ye don't like your tea wi'out milk."

"Eigh, it won't matter," she said.

She began warming the milk in water.

"I often think we just do things fro' habit, Dan," she went on. "They say i' China, now, they always drink tea wi'out milk."

"Happen it's because they haven't learned any better," he mumbled.

He kept on rubbing the dog's cold body as his wife

stirred the milk in the pan on the grate. There was silence in the cottage.

Lassie lay there, unmoving. In her half-conscious-ness and terrible weariness, a feeling of dim peace stole over her. So many things came from the past and com-forted her. The place smelled "right." There was the mixed aroma of coal-smoke and baking bread. The hands that touched her—they did not imprison or bring pain. Instead they soothed and brought peace to sore and aching muscles. The people—they did not move suddenly or shout noisily or throw things that hurt. They went quietly, not startling a dog.

There was warmth, too—this most of all. It was a drugging warmth, one which dulled the senses and made awareness slip away as if in a gentle stream that flowed on to forgetfulness and death.

Only dimly Lassie knew of the saucer of warm milk set beside her head. Her senses would not come back from their half-conscious state. She tried to lift her head but it would not move. Then she felt her head being lifted. The warm milk was being spooned down her throat. She gulped, once—twice—three times. The trickle of hotness went into her body. It finished the lulling of her senses. She lay still, and the milk now being spooned into her mouth dribbled out again and onto the rug.

In the cottage the woman rose and stood beside her husband. "D'ye think it's dying, Dan? It doesn't swal-low any more."

"I don't know, Dally. It may live the night. We've done the best we can. All we can do is just—let it be."

The woman stared at it.

"Dan, I think I'll sit up wi' it."

"Now, Dally. Ye've done your best, and . . ."

"But it might need some help and . . . it's such a bonnie dog, Dan."

"Bonnie! That ugly mongrel of a stray . . ."

"Oh, Dan. It's the bonniest dog I ever saw."

Firmly the old woman planted herself in the rocking chair and settled herself for a night of watching.

A week later Mrs. Fadden sat in her chair. The morning sunlight streamed through the window, and the memory of the storm seemed like a dream of long ago. She looked over her glasses and beamed at Lassie, lying on the rug, her ears erect. "It's himself," she said aloud. "And ye know it, don't ye?"

There came the footsteps of her husband, and then the door opened.

"Ye know, Dan, she knows your footsteps already," the woman said proudly.

"Ah," he said skeptically.

"She does," Dally maintained. "The other day, when that pedlar came, she just raised the roof, I'll tell ye. My word, she let him know someone was home while ye were in town! But she doesn't make a sound when she hears you coming—so she must know your footsteps."

"Ah," the man replied again.

"She's smart—and she's bonnie," the woman said—more to the dog than to the man. "Isn't she bonnie, Dan?"

"Aye, that she is."

"And first off ye said she was ugly."

"Aye, but that was before . . ."

"See, I just took an old comb and did her coat all pretty."

They looked at Lassie, now lying with head erect in that lion-like posture that collies so often take. Her slim muzzle was held gracefully above the ruff that once again was beginning to show glossy white.

"Doesn't she look different?" the woman asked proudly.

"Aye, that's it, Dally," the man said dolefully.

The woman caught his ominous tone.

"Well, what's the matter?"

"Eigh, Dally. Ye see, that's just it. First off, I thought she was a mongrel. But now . . . well, she's a fine dog."

"Of course she's a fine dog," the old woman said happily. "All she needed was a bit o' warmth and a little to eat and somebody to be kind to her."

The man shook his head as if exasperated at his wife who did not see what he was driving at.

"Aye, but don't ye understand, Dally? She's a fine dog—and now she's all cleaned up and getting better, ye can see she's a very valuable dog. And . . ."

"And what?"

"Well, a valuable dog will have owners somewhere."

"Owners? Fine owners who'd leave a poor thing out wandering and bony and starving on a night like we took her in. Owners, indeed!"

The man shook his head and sat in his chair heavily. He stuffed his clay pipe.

"No, Dally, it's no good. She's a valuable dog, and I can see it now. So don't get your heart set on her, because any day the owner might come . . ."

The woman sat, her mind worrying over this new and terrible thought. Her beautiful dog—*her* dog!

She stared at the fire and then, for a long time, at Lassie. Finally she spoke: "Well then, if this has got to be taken away fro' us, Dan—it might as well be sooner as later. Oh, if anyone owns it! Find out, will ye, Dan? Go ask around."

The man nodded. "It's honest," he said. "I'll go to town and ask around tomorrow."

"No, Dan, today. Go right now. For I'd never have a

minute's peace nor sleep a wink till I knew. Go today and ask around everywhere, and then if she's to go, she'll go. And if nobody owns her, then we've done our duty and can rest easy."

The man puffed his pipe, but the woman gave him no rest until he agreed to go that day.

At noon he set out, walking slowly down the road to the town four miles away. All through the afternoon the woman rocked. Sometimes she went to the door and looked down the highway.

It was a long afternoon. The minutes dragged for the old woman. It was falling dusk when at last she heard the footsteps. Almost before the door opened she began:

"Well?"

"I asked all around the place—everywhere—and nobody seems to ha' lost her."

"Then she's ours!"

The woman beamed with joy and looked at the proud dog, still thin and pinched, but to her the perfection of canine breeding.

"She's ours," she repeated. "We gave them their chance. Now she's ours."

"Well, now, Dally. They might pass by chance and see her, so don't . . ."

"She's ours now," the woman repeated stolidly.

Mentally she was resolving that no owner should pass and ever see the dog. She would see to that. The dog should stay always beside her in the cottage. She would not have it running around loose outside for that terrible, unknown owner to see as he passed by!

The Noblest Gift—Freedom

Lassie lay on the rug. Strength had returned to her in the three weeks she had been in her new home. Her senses were back to normal, and her muscles were almost as strong as ever.

Other things had come back to her, too. When she had been weak and ill, these had been like forgotten things. But now they grew each day with the return of her health—insistent and demanding.

The one driving force of her life was wakened, and it was leaving her no peace.

It always grew worse in the afternoon. As the clock moved round toward four, it became maddening.

It was the time sense.

It was time—time to go—time to go for the boy!

Lassie rose and went to the door. She whined and lifted her head.

"Ah, now, girl!"

It was the old woman.

"Ye've been out for a nice walk wi' me, on the string! Ye don't need to go out again. So come back here and rest yourself."

But Lassie did not obey. She poked with her muzzle at the door. She walked to the window and stood on her hind legs. She dropped to all fours and went back to the door. Then, like an animal in a cage, she began pacing back and forth. She kept it up endlessly, walking to the door and turning, walking to the window and turning. She kept it up, her feet padding on the stone floor of the cottage. The click of her paw-nails went as rhythmically as the click of the old woman's knitting needles.

An hour later, Lassie ended her patrol. Slowly she went to the hearth rug. The time was past. She lay down and regarded the fire with unblinking eyes.

Animals are creatures of habit—but new habits can be formed. There was a real chance that Lassie would forget and become contented in her new home. The couple treated her with all the love of their simple life, and she obeyed them and came to them when they called and allowed them to stroke and fondle her.

But she did it with the forbearance of a dog that has only one master—and he is absent.

For Lassie did not forget. Instead, with her returning health, she remembered more and more, and her daily patrollings in the late afternoon became longer and more agitated.

Nor did the old couple fail to notice it. The old woman who so treasured this new thing of affection that had come into her life was aware of every move that Lassie made. Such a steady occurrence as Lassie's afternoon pacing between the window and the door could not be disregarded.

The woman hoped, and almost dreamed, that the dog would forget the outside world and be content in their small, snug, humble world of the cottage and the chickens and the goose. But finally she realized that it was no use, for Lassie began to refuse her food. Then the old woman knew.

She sat long one evening and at last, out of the silence, she spoke.

"Dan!"

"What is it now?"

"She's not happy here."

"Happy? Who isn't—what're ye talking about?"

"You know what I'm talking about. Herself. She's not happy. She's fretting."

"Oh, now nonsense. Ye think more o' that dog. Every time Herself winks an eyebrow, ye're thinking she's got the measles or the plague or—I don't know what."

The woman turned her eyes on Herself—as they had christened Lassie. She shook her head.

"No I didn't tell you, but the last three days, Dan, she's not eating."

The man lifted his glasses to his forehead and studied the dog. Then his regard came to his aged wife.

"Now, now, Dally. It's all right. Ye've been feeding her so much I don't wonder she'd turn her nose up at a dinner fit for a king. That's all."

"No, it's not nonsense, Dan. And well you know it. For why do ye always keep her so tight on a string when ye take her out last thing at night?"

"Well, that's just in case—well, till she gets used to this as her home. If I let her free, she might get lost, and not knowing this countryside well, wouldn't find her way back, and . . ."

"Ah, ye know that's a tale, Dan. As well as I do, ye know that if she was free she'd be away and leaving us alone here, and never coming back."

The man did not answer. The woman went on.

"She's not happy, Dan. Ye don't see her as I do— every afternoon, window to door, door to window, until I think she'll wear a path deep in the flagging . . ."

"Oh, now, that's just a dog's way of asking to go for a walk."

"It is not, Dan. For I've tried it. I take her on the string—and not that she doesn't follow bonnie and mind me. But she does it, Dan—ye know what I think?"

"What?"

"Well, like she's just doing it because she's sorry for us. We've been kind to her, and she wouldn't want to hurt our feelings, so she just puts up with us. Like she's too polite to run unless we tell her to go . . ."

"Ah, now, no dog can be full of things like that—like human things . . ."

"Nay, my Herself is, Dan. Ye don't know that dog. Dan!"

"Well?"

The old woman's voice dropped.

"Ye see, I know about this dog. I know something."

"What?"

"Dan, she's going somewhere. She's on her way."

"Ah, now, woman, and what fancies are ye building in your mind!"

"I don't care, Dan. I know—me and Herself, we both know. She was on her way, Dan, and she got tired on the way and she'd just stopped here like it was a hospital—or a wayside inn in a story. And now she's better, she wants to be on her way. But she's so polite and understanding, she doesn't want to hurt us. But in her heart she's for being away. She's not happy here."

The old man did not answer. He tapped out his clay pipe in the palm of his hand and looked steadily at the dog. Finally he spoke.

"Aye," he said. "All right, Dally. All right."

There are people whose hearts are so full of ugly fear that when they see a thirsty animal pass with a fleck of saliva on its parched jowl, they must run in terror shouting, "Mad dog!" There are others to whom every passing creature is an enemy, to be harried on its way with a flung stone. But, and for this the canine

world must be thankful, there are others with affection
and deep understanding in their lives who bring dignity
and honor to the relationship between man and dog.

Such was the old couple, who on the next afternoon
sat watching the dog. When the time neared four
o'clock, and Lassie rose, their eyes followed her.

And when Lassie whined at the door and then paced
to the window, they both sighed.

"Well," the old man said.

'That was all. They both got up. The woman opened
the door. Side by side, the old man and his wife followed Lassie out to the road.

There for a moment, the dog stood, as if unable to
realize that at last her great urge could be fulfilled. She
looked back at the woman whose hands had patted and
fondled her and fed her.

For a second, the old woman wished to call—to call
the dog back to her and try again to wean its mind
from old memories. But she was too honest. She lifted
her head, and her aged voice came clearly.

"It's all right, then, dog. If ye must go—awa' wi'
ye."

In that sentence, Lassie caught the word "go." It
was what she wanted. She turned, looked back once as
in a glance of farewell, and then started—not up the
road to the east, nor down to the west, but straight
across the field. She was going south again.

She went at a trot—the same trot that had carried
her bravely through the Highlands of Scotland. Not a
fast one, nor a slow one, but a steady pace that ate at
miles, that could be kept up for hour after hour. So she
went, across the field, over a wall, and down the slope.

Back on the road, the old woman stood, her chin set
firm. And she waved her hand and said:

"Good-bye, Herself. Good-bye—and good luck to
ye."

Long after the dog was out of sight she stood there, and her husband put his arm around her.

"It's getting rare chilly, now, Dally," he said. "We'd better go in."

They went into the cottage, and the routine of life went on. The woman prepared the simple evening meal. She lit the lamp. They sat at the table.

But neither of them ate.

Then the man looked up and said sympathetically.

"I'll put the lamp in the window, Dally, for tonight. Like, for chance, she's just gone for a long run. And then if she wants to find her way back . . ."

He knew the dog was never coming back, but he had thought it might make his wife feel better if he told her this. However, he stopped speaking, for as he looked up he saw his wife's head bowed, and tears were falling. Quickly he rose.

"Now, now, Dally," he said. "Now, now!"

He put his arms about her and patted her consolingly.

"Eigh, now don't fret yourself, Dally. Look, I'll tell ye what. I've a couple of shillings put away, and I'll take down a few eggs and sell 'em—and then I'll go to the market, and I know a place where they sell dogs. And I'll get ye another. Eh? A fine little dog that'll stay here wi' ye, and not want to run away.

"Ah, Herself was too big, she was—and them big ones eat too much anyhow—and, and . . . a nice little one . . ."

The old woman looked up. She wanted to cry out the words that always come from a dog lover after his animal is gone: "I don't ever want another dog!"

But because of regard for her husband she never spoke the words.

"Aye, it cost a lot to feed, Dan."

"O' course it did. And a little dog—or perhaps a

cat—why, it'd cost almost nothing . . ."

"That's it, a cat, Dan! If ye'd get me just a nice cat."

"Aye—one that'd stay curled up on the hearth and stay by ye. That's it! I'll find ye a fine cat—the finest cat anybody could ever want. How's that?"

The old woman looked up.

"Ah, Daniel, ye're kind to me."

Then she dashed her tears away and smiled.

"Eigh, sure. We're getting all in a stew—and here's tea getting all cold," he said.

"Oh, I couldn't eat, Dan."

"Well, then, have a nice cup o' tea."

"Aye, that's so," she said. "A good cup o' tea'll cheer us both up."

"It will, indeed. And Saturday—we'll have you the bonniest little cat ye ever did see. Won't that be fine?"

The woman smiled bravely.

"Aye, it'll be fine," she said.

On The Road with Rowlie

Rowlie Palmer finished shaving and cleaned off his old-fashioned straight razor. He was a little, cheery man with a red face that somehow seemed full of buttons. His eyes were like buttons, his weather-beaten lips were like buttons, there were odd bumps and warts on his forehead and chin that were like buttons.

The button-similarity went into actual practice in his clothes. He wore a knitted woolen overshirt, which was dotted with pearl-shell buttons at every available place. Over that he wore a curious corduroy jacket with leather sleeves, and on that were numerous brass buttons which, if one had inspected closer, would have shown plainly as one-time fasteners of tunics in His Majesty's army.

Rowlie's face and form were well known throughout the north of England, for he was a traveling potter. He lived in the horse-drawn wagon caravan that carried his goods and traveled slowly along the roads. When he came to a village or town, he would take out a stout cudgel and begin to beat one of his largest pottery bowls—an enormous thing of brown and yellow glaze. The result would be a sound like the rich-toned chiming of a great bell.

And Rowlie would lift up his voice and chant: "Here comes Pedlar Palmer, the Potter.

Bowls and pots, I've got lots!
Bring your penny or you won't get any!
Bowls and pots!"

He loved to make his grand entrances into the small towns of the north, banging vigorously with a great show on the pottery bowl. He always belabored it proudly for the double reason—to signal his coming and to show how stout was his ware that could not be broken by even such lusty blows.

Once a year he covered his route. When his stock got low, he would circle back to his home village where his older brother, Mark, made the pottery. Mark would look up and nod from his potter's wheel in the great shed where he fashioned the old-fashioned utensils. Rowlie would stock up again with the wares: tiny ones small enough for a child's bowl of porridge up to the great ones nearly three feet across, which the northern housewives loved to use for kneeding their bread dough—and often for washing the baby in. He would load his van with the brown-and-yellow things, so shining with their crude glazes, and off he would go again. "Well—I'm off," he would say.

Mark would look up and nod—and go on working.

Then away Rowlie would start on his route, traveling by day, at night pulling Bess over to the side of the road by a good camping place.

It was a comfortable, happy life. For in his van, Rowlie had a complete home. It was incredible that in such a small space so full a life could be achieved just by compactness. Often as a great favor to a customer Rowlie would let him see the living quarters. And even the best housewives, looking in, would exclaim over the spotlessness of the van.

There was a place for everything. A place for the razor that Rowlie was putting away. A place for his washbowl. A tiny rail for his towel.

His cot was made, his breakfast finished, his dishes put away. Bess was harnessed, her oat bag slung beneath the cart. Rowlie got to the seat.

"Hi, up, Bess!" he cried.

Once out on the road, Rowlie jumped down from the seat of his moving van and began walking alongside it. Bess had enough to pull without his extra weight. And he loved to walk, unless the weather was too bad.

But the weather was good now. Rowlie went along, with the half-mist of morning still hanging to the ground, singing:

> Oh, father, father, dig my grave,
> And dig it with your garden spade,
> And place on top a turtle-dove,
> To show them that I died for love.

It was a sad song, but Rowlie did not mind that. In fact, he never realized it. It was just that in his lonesome life his own voice kept him company from town to town. He had no other company but Bess, the horse, and Toots. And Toots—she was a one, as Rowlie would put it. She sat on the seat now—a tiny white dog, which might have been poodle, fox terrier, Pomeranian, or Skye terrier; but was all of them.

Toots was almost as well known as Rowlie. She could stand on her hind legs on an inverted bowl and balance another smaller bowl on her nose. She could jump on a ball of wood and roll it by walking along, still balancing. She could pick up pennies from the ground and bring them to Rowlie. She could jump through hoops.

Whenever Rowlie reached a good village, he would put on a show with Toots—not as a mountebank might, to collect pence, but because he enjoyed the laughter and happiness of the children who gathered there.

Between towns Toots sat primly in the driver's seat as she sat now, regarding the road as Rowlie sang his doleful story of the hapless village maiden.

His mind was not on the words. Instead, as always, his senses were alert to the world about him. Traveling and living in the open as he did, Rowlie knew a good deal about his world. He knew where magpies nested and when the swallows came and went. And no huntsman in the land had an eye any quicker than Rowlie's for seeing the whisp of red that was a fox.

So this morning, his senses were alert, and his eyes flicked over a field, and his song halted. He walked over beside his moving cart and stood on the step beside the shafts. Thus he rode, his body pressed against the front of his vehicle. As he went, he watched. It was a dog, coming steadily across the field, veering toward the road.

She came without halting—as if a horse-drawn van was a thing of nature, like a tree or a deer. Rowlie knew that and so kept his body out of sight. Only he muttered to himself:

"Now what are ye up to, eh?"

Nearer the dog came, until, by a part of unfenced moorland, it slipped to the road, just as the cart passed.

"Well, and what do ye want?" Rowlie said out loud.

The dog looked up and recrossed the ditch into the moorland.

"Don't like my company, eh?" Rowlie said.

He got down from the step and began walking again. His eyes followed the dog, now going ahead and to his left, yet traveling almost parallel. But its passage was stopped by a stream. It began moving back to the road again, where it could cross on the bridge.

Rowlie clambered into his cart, and when he came out he had in his hand a few small pieces of liver. Toots lifted her nose and wagged her nondescript tail.

"It's not for thee, my lass," Rowlie said.

He kept his eye on the dog. It would arrive at the bridge just as his wagon did.

"Well, we'll pretend not to notice thee this time," he said aloud.

He began singing, lustily:

> *My old feyther, he used to say to me,*
> *Now here's a bit o' good advice I'm bahn to give*
>   *to thee.*
> *Th'art so simple, so varry varry dense . . .*

And then—

"Ah-gee-way, there Bess. No, not right into th' ditch. Ah-gee-whoa a bit. That's it!"

And—

> *Thy yead is full o' summat*
> *But it isn't full o' sense.*
> *Th' only time th'art intelligent at all . . .*

So singing, timing the speed of his horse, Rowlie arrived at the bridge as the dog drew near. He went on singing lustily, pretending not to notice it. The dog halted, as if to let him pass first. Rowlie did not turn his head. Instead he waved the pieces of liver in his hand so that the scent scattered in the air. Unconcernedly he dropped one. Then he passed over the bridge. Half turning his head, he looked to see what the dog would do.

Behind, by the bridge, Lassie walked slowly to the piece of meat. The aroma of it seemed to fill the air. Her hunger drove the saliva glands to work and her

mouth filled with wetness. She walked nearer. She bent
her nose to touch the meat.

But training of years was there, too. How carefully
had Sam Carraclough taught her not to pick up strange
food. He had done that by dropping small pieces of
meat at various places—and in the meat was inserted
cores of burning red pepper. As a pup Lassie had
started to eat those bits and had soon discovered that
they contained what seemed to be balls of living flame.
Moreover, as her mouth burned, she had been scolded
by the voice of her master.

"It's a cruel hard thing to do," Sam Carraclough had
told his son Joe, "but it's t'only way I know that can
teach 'em—and I'd sooner have a pup taste hot pepper
than have a raised dog dying o' poisoned meat some
madman has thrown to it."

And that lesson had stayed with Lassie.

A dog must not eat stray bits of food!

Yet the hunger in her was something that went back
before training. Her nose trembled. She nuzzled the
piece of liver. Then suddenly she wheeled. She left the
meat and crossed the bridge.

Ahead of her Rowlie Palmer, by his wagon, nodded
his head.

"A good tyke and a well-brought-up one," he said.
"Good for thee, my tyke. But we'll see . . ."

He walked on singing, but still waving liver in the air
so that he left what was to a dog a great, broad, rich
swathe of delectable aroma.

And in that smell of desired food, Lassie now
traveled. Once over the bridge, her impulse was to
leave the road again and go through the fields. But she
did not want to leave the trail of this sweet-smelling
food. She trotted along, crossed the ditch, and began
traveling slightly to the rear and parallel to the van in
the road.

Rowlie Palmer sang merrily to Toots on the seat:

> *There's a tyke that's shy and canny,*
> *But I think she's coming near.*
> *Aye, she may be fearfu' canny,*
> *But we'll overcome her fear.*

"How's that for a rhyme, Toots? Eh, ye'd like a companion. Well, we'll see."

So Rowlie Palmer traveled along his road. Sometimes, when he turned his head, he could see the collie in the fields behind him. Sometimes she was lost to view and gone for quite a length of time. But always she would be back again, drawn to the scent of meat, following it steadily. And each time she came back she would come a bit nearer the wagon and the man who seemed to pay not the slightest heed in the world to her.

So it went all through the morning, as they crossed flat, bleak lands. As the sun was high, Rowlie Palmer pulled off the road. He saw the dog halt behind him.

"Time for a bite, Toots," he said.

Quickly he set up a small brazier and built a fire. He boiled water and made tea. He warmed over a pot of stew. He cut up liver and put it down in a bowl for Toots. He ate. All the time he watched the collie, drawing nearer and nearer. Very ostentatiously, he fed bits of food to his little dog. He saw the collie, now sitting only twenty feet away, following with its eyes every move that his hands made. Toots barked at her, shrilly, once or twice, but Rowlie quieted his pet promptly.

When at last his meal was done, he rose.

"Now," he said, "we know a trick or two, don't we, Toots? And we'll see whether ye'll eat or not."

He took from his stock a flat bowl. He filled it with

bits of liver. As unconcerned as if it was something he had done every day for years, he walked halfway to the collie and set the bowl down.

"There's your dinner," he said. "Eat it up."

Lassie watched him go back to the brazier. Then, as he seemed to be taking no notice of her, she rose from her sitting position. Slowly she walked to the bowl.

A dog must not eat stray bits of food!

But this was different. It wasn't stray. It was set out in a bowl. That was it. It was in a bowl. And when a bowl or plate was set out by man, that meant a dog could eat without fear. There would be no living fire inside the food.

Gently Lassie dropped her head. With her front teeth, she lifted a piece of meat. She snapped it upwards. Then in the joy of eating again, she tore into the food. She cleaned up the bowl. She licked the bowl itself. Then she sat, looking at the man, as if to say:

"Well, for an appetizer that was all right. Now where's the real meal?"

Rowlie shook his head and spoke out loud.

"Ah, no. Ye'll come along wi' me if ye want any more. Didn't I say we knew a thing or two about tykes, Toots? Put it down in the road, and it's no go! Somebody trained thee too well, my collie friend. But put it down in a bowl—that was the secret. That made it all right. Well, up we get and on our way!"

He took off Bess' nosebag. He tipped his brazier and stamped out the fire carefully. Snugly he stowed everything away. All the time from the corner of his eye, he saw the collie, sitting, as if waiting to see whether the miracle of a fine dinner would happen all over again. And when at last he started and was on the road again, Rowlie Palmer grunted happily. For the collie was traveling with him; not in the field now, but close behind the van. It was not too close—but Rowlie didn't mind that. That would come later he very well knew.

He sang merrily:

> They'll hang me by the neck till I am dead,
> Yes, they'll hang me by the neck till I am dead,
>   They'll take me from my bed,
>   To the gallows I'll be led,
>   And I'll hang till I am dead—blast your eyes!

Days later, Lassie was still with Rowlie Palmer. She trotted by the road, always a few feet behind the pottery van. Rowlie tried to teach her to swing along under the wagon behind the rear axle, as a well-trained Dalmatian carriage dog would have done in the days of traps and phaetons; but Lassie would have none of it.

She never liked the banging and shouting as they came into villages, but it was as if she put up with it, knowing it could not last long. She was content as long as Rowlie went south. Once, at a fork in the road, Rowlie turned his van east. Some sense told him that part of his animal family was missing. He looked back. Lassie was sitting at the road junction.

Every time he called to her, she came a few steps, then circled, went back, and sat down.

Finally Rowlie threw up his hands. He climbed to the seat of the van, turned Bess around and started south on the other fork.

"Eigh, I can just as well go round Godsey way as by Menlip," he said affably.

But later he turned to Toots.

"Ye see what a poor thing a man is among women. Thee and Bess and Her Majesty. What chance has one lone male got again' the three of ye? Bess wants to go north 'cause that's home. Her Majesty wants to go south—for the winter on the Rivveyeria, no doubt. And thee—eigh, tha's content as long as tha's wi' me.

Aye, Toots, tha's the only one that loves me for masen
alone!"

And the little dog wagged its tail that was neither
curly nor straight nor short-haired nor plumed.

It was a good life, traveling along the unfrequented
lanes of the north country, far from the main highways
where the trucks and lorries and motorcars that Rowlie
hated so much went racing along. And Rowlie sang as
the miles passed.

"Well, Your Majesty. Shall us common folks do a
little vulgar business?"

Rowlie addressed the words to Lassie behind the
wagon. She walked along, giving no sign of having
heard.

"I know, Your Majesty," Rowlie said humbly. "It
does hurt your royal ears to hear me speak of such
things as money, but us humbler folks has got to live,
so if ye don't mind—if ye don't mind—me and Toots
will earn a little money."

Delighted with his own make-believe, Rowlie lifted
his cap to Lassie and bowed low. Then he turned to his
wagon and took down the largest bowl and his cudgel.
He banged lustily as he approached the first house.

The bell-like din echoed in the village. Rowlie's
voice lifted:

> *Bowls and pots, I've got lots,*
> *Bring your penny or ye won't get any!*
> *Bowls and pots!*

The women flocked to the doors, and Rowlie greeted
them. He halted his wagon by the village center, while
the housewives fingered his wares and argued and
joked about prices.

"They're so strong ye can't break 'em!" Rowlie chanted.

"I broke the one I got fro' ye last year," a woman cried.

"Well, I have to have 'em break once in a while," Rowlie said, his eyes gleaming. "If I made 'em absolutely unbreakable, ye'd never want any new ones and I'd do myself out of a job."

He winked broadly, and the women screamed with laughter and nudged each other and said:

"Eigh, he's a one, that Pedlar Potter Palmer!"

"Now," Rowlie said, when the buying was done. "Who wants to see the tyke do a few tricks?"

The children yelled and clapped their hands. Rowlie got out the paraphernalia from the wagon and set it up. Toots scrambled nimbly from the seat. Rowlie clapped his hands. But nothing happened. The little dog sat waiting.

"What's the matter?" Rowlie said. "Ye're waiting for someone? Eigh, I see. Her Majesty hasn't arrived for the command performance. Why, here she comes now."

Carefully trained by Rowlie, Lassie strolled before the crowd and sat down. Rowlie gave her a little bit of liver as her reward. "Well, now Her Majesty's here at last, we can begin, can't we?" Rowlie pattered on.

At the signal with his hand, Toots barked excitedly and began her routine. She jumped through the hoops. She told how old she was by barking. She played "dead dog." She picked out the prettiest girl in the crowd—all by Rowlie's hidden signals. Then she ended with her best trick, walking on the ball of wood while she carried in her mouth a tiny national flag.

"Doesn't the collie do aught?" a child cried.

"Why, ye wouldn't expect royalty to perform, would

ye?" Rowlie answered. "But it does seem like she's on a sit-down strike."

Rowlie advanced to Lassie, carrying Toots in his arms.

"Would ye like to do some work?" he asked.

Lassie sat unblinking.

"Would ye like to pick up the things after the star's finished?"

Lassie still sat.

"Pick up those things!" Rowlie ordered in a thunderous tone.

Lassie did not move, and the children screamed happily. Rowlie scratched his head in mock dismay. Then his eye brightened. He held up his finger to the children. Then he turned to Lassie.

"May it please Your Majesty, but as a favor to me, would ye please pick up the things?"

This time he gave the signal with his hand—for the words had no bearing on the trick—and Lassie rose proudly. She pushed the wooden ball with her slim muzzle to the van. She picked up the hoops one by one and set them in a pile by the door. Rowlie bowed to her. Lassie curtsied, stretching her front legs forward stiffly as a dog does after it has been sleeping.

"Ye see," Rowlie said to the children. "Always remember to say please, and ye'll get more in this world. Well. Off we go. Don't forget Pedlar Palmer the Potter. I'll be back next year. Good-bye," he called, waving.

The hands fluttered in the village, and away went the caravan. Rowlie sang happily. Toots coiled up snugly on the front seat. Bess plodded along at her steady amble. Lassie trotted unconcernedly behind. She was glad they were on the road again. She disliked the halts in the villages, and she never really liked the performances in which she played such a small part.

She was unlike Toots, who delighted in the tricks and could hardly wait to go through them. Toots was a born trick dog. Lassie—she was not of that kind.

Rowlie Palmer knew that. He looked at Toots who lay half asleep.

"Aye, she's a fine dog fro' somewhere—but she'll never be as smart as thee, my sweetheart, will she?"

Toots gave an agitated squirm that was meant to be a wagging of the tail.

Rowlie finished the evening meal and made his caravan ready again.

"Aye, I know. Ye don't want to turn out again," he said to Bess. "But it's a long jump this time, and we'll get some o' the road under our feet. It's clear enough."

Rowlie turned his eyes upward again. There was a clear moon, but there was a crispness in the air, too.

"Really mucky weather ahead if I know it—and then winter'll be down on us—and we've got to head back toward home. So we'll put on steam a bit and get some miles done tonight."

He turned his wagon out on the road, and soon there was the steady clop-clop of Bess's hooves on the flinty way. Toots slept soundly on the front seat. Happy to be on the way again, Lassie trotted at the rear of the caravan.

Rowlie was counting in his mind. A good four hours more, and long before ten o'clock, he should be at that snug camping place beside the Apden woods. It would be cold by then. A nice cup of tea over the brazier to cheer him up and then to bed, and up and off with the sun tomorrow morning.

A Gallant Heart—and a Good-bye

The two men came up along the road where the trees cast deep gloom from the moonlight.

"Well, if ye don't like it, Snickers, ye know what ye can do!" The man who spoke was a great, thickset man. His shoulders bulged under his moleskin jacket. The peaked cap came down over a broad, square-jowled face. The man he addressed was smaller, thin faced. From the tip of his long nose hung a small crystal, which seemed to be ever there, no matter how much he sniffed.

"Ye give me a pain, ye does, Snickers—allus grousing. 'Ere I lets yer be my pal—I lets yer travel with me—I fair sees ye live on the bloomin' fat o' the land, and what do I get for it? Grouse, grouse, grouse all the time. Yer tired, ye are; yer feet 'urt yer, they do; yer cold, ye are! Why, ye bloomin' . . ."

"Buckles, look!"

The big man halted his tirade and looked where the other pointed. Through the gloom there was a glimmer of warm light. Buckles wiped the back of his hand slowly over his mouth. He looked about. By the roadside he saw a stout branch of wood. He unclasped his knife and hacked viciously, trimming away the rough ends of limb. Finally he was satisfied. He balanced the cudgel in his hand. He saw Snicker had done the same.

Not a word had been spoken. Buckles merely mo-

tioned with his head, and the two stole silently down
the road. Five minutes later they were lying in a
thicket. The smell of burning wood came straight into
their faces.

"Pedlar Palmer the Potter," Snickers whispered,
reading the sign on the van. "A bloomin' traveling
'awker, that's what."

"'Awker," Buckles breathed. "Then 'e'll have it with
him."

"That 'e will, Buckles. They carries it wiv 'em."

"Come on, then!"

Buckles rose and began a stealthy advance. But before he had gone ten paces the still night was torn with
the deep challenge of a dog, sounding a throaty alarm.

"'E's got a dog," Snickers panted.

"What do I care?" Buckles said.

He stepped out boldly, now that concealment was
gone, and advanced to the place where the fire glowed
in the brazier.

"'Old yer dog, mate. It's all right. We ain't doin'
nuthin'," Buckles called.

As he came to the fire, Lassie bayed. He motioned
at her with his club, but she faded away. Rowlie tried
to grasp her, but she eluded him, too, and stood at the
circle of the fire growling. And now Toots's shrill yapping rose to add to the din.

"Quiet!" Rowlie said. "Quiet, both of ye."

The dogs subsided to a rumble. Then Buckles
grinned. He heard Snickers standing behind him.

"That's good, o' ye, mate," Buckles went on, in what
he meant to be a disarming, friendly tone. "What ye
'aving, tea? Now ain't that nice. Could ye just spare a
couple of 'omeless chaps looking for work a swaller or
two to warm 'em up?"

He advanced, smiled.

Rowlie rose from his seat on the log. Despite Buckles' words, he was not fooled. He had not traveled alone for so many years without learning to read the character, or lack of it, of men he met in lonesome places.

"No, yer don't!" Buckles shouted.

He leaped between Rowlie and the van toward which the pedlar had been edging. He balanced the cudgel, smiling. Now all pretence was gone.

"Come on, where is it?" he said coaxingly. "Because if yer nice and 'ands it over wivout any trouble, we won't 'urt ye, will we, Snickers?"

"No, we won't 'urt 'im."

"Of course, we won't. But—if ye want trouble, then, sorry as we are, of course, we'll give it to yer. Come on! Where is it?"

"Why, I'll give it to ye, " Rowlie began.

Then he broke off his own words, and with a sudden leap was beside his caravan. Now in his hand rested his own stout stick. He placed his back against the van. He spit on his hands. He did not speak, nor did he need to.

"So, ye want it the 'ard way, do ye?" Buckles breathed. "Well, all right."

He lashed out with his weapon. Rowlie parried it and slashed backhanded in return, catching the big man's knuckles. Buckles roared in anger.

"Come on, Snickers, don't stand there—get round the other side of 'im, ye bloomin' coward."

The two men rushed in together, and Rowlie, against the van, tried to keep them beyond the half circle of his reach. The blows began to fall on his head and shoulders. He was helpless.

In despair, he looked at Lassie, now baying beyond the campfire. "Come on, get 'em," he called.

Lassie darted about, then suddenly rushed at the bigger man. He turned and smashed at her with his stick. The blow fell across her shoulder, almost rolling her over. For a second the fight stopped and the men turned to the dog. They saw her stand, looking at them.

In Lassie's mind there were conflicting impulses. But one rose to the top.

Here again were men whose hands meant evil, who could reach out to hurt and give pain. These were hands that would capture and imprison. These were the men to avoid as she had done so many times before. A dog should slip away and not be seen by them.

At that moment, Buckles made a half step toward Lassie, raising his club.

"Go on," he shouted. "Before I give yer another."

Lassie slid away. Then she turned into the underbrush and trotted up the slope into the woods.

Buckles turned back to Rowlie.

"What a dog!" he roared. "Ye see, mate—even yer best friend won't stick by yer. Oh, what a bloomin' dog that is! Now come on, 'and it over peaceful like, and we'll let bygones be bygones."

Rowlie's eyes, which had followed Lassie up into the woods, turned back to the men. He spit on his hands again. He braced himself.

"Come and get it," he said stubbornly.

The men crept closer, swinging warily at Rowlie. They stepped about cautiously in the firelight, for the pedlar was no weakling, and with his back against the van could keep a semicircle clear before him. And as he fought, parrying and replying deftly with his club, the tiny dog, Toots, scurried about, true to her trust, defending her master.

It was pitifully little that the tiny dog could do—almost laughable the way she darted about, yapping and shrilling, a little white bundle of energy. Grimly she dashed in, and at last managed to get her tiny teeth into the ankle of the big attacker.

In a second of surprise Buckles shook the dog loose with a kick of his foot.

"Ye bloomin' little rat," he said.

The little dog rushed in again, and Buckles, lifting his great cudgel, smote with all his strength. The small body was knocked, lifeless and broken, into the underbrush.

Shouting in mad anger at what he had seen, Rowlie charged out, driving the men back with his frenzied onslaught. He swung the club in fury, and seemed as if he would drive the men before him.

For a few moments they were swept back; but then Rowlie's anger proved his own undoing, for he had left the protection of the van and now was attacked on both sides. Buckles, aching from the savage blows of the pedlar's club, beat down Rowlie's guard, and a crushing blow on the shoulder sent the potter to his knees. Trying to rise, he covered his head with his stick and crooked arm. He felt a blow from the rear. Turning, he clutched Snickers and hung onto the man. He would make one enemy shield him from the other until his senses cleared. He felt a trickle of warm blood coming down into his left eye and knew his scalp was badly cut.

When Lassie first vanished into the underbrush at the threat of Buckles' club, she trotted away from the fire and automatically headed south.

Yet, as she went, she no longer felt the peaceful calm that always came when she was making headway in the desired direction. Somehow—something was wrong.

She halted in her tracks and looked back. Now, barely visible through the trees, was the glow of the fire, and her ears caught plainly the cries of the men and the shrilling of Toots. It was that high yapping that seemed to call her more than anything else, for it was the alarm—a dog crying rage and defiance.

Lassie circled, gliding through the brush, and went back. At last she sat on the bank. Toot's cries sounded no more. Lassie could see the men staggering about before their giant shadows. She saw Rowlie sink to the ground.

There were two opposing forces struggling in Lassie—one to keep away from men; the other to defend her home. For the van and the campfire were her home in a sense. And this latter force was the older one in her—one that went back to her ancestors. Her shyness of men was a later thing, acquired only in the last few months of her life. And suddenly the older force won.

She had never attacked man in her life, and she was not a ferocious breed. Yet, once the conviction held her, she did not hesitate, nor did she go warily. With a deep, ugly baying that came from her chest, with her hackles raised, she started down the bank.

The first that the men about the fire knew of the dog's return was when a furry shape came across the patch of light from the fire like a thunderbolt. She sailed through the air, striking Buckles in the chest. The force of the first charge toppled the big man over. Lassie did not stop. She went out of the circle of light, wheeled through the brush, and came back in another direction. She raced past Snickers, still clutched by Rowlie, and slashed with her teeth into his leg as she passed.

The force of her drive tore her fangs through the flesh, and the night was broken by Snickers' scream of pain.

She turned to Buckles again.

"So, ye're back," he muttered.

Confident that she would run as before, he charged at her. But Lassie this time ducked the swing of the

club and raced past, tearing the calf of the man's leg.
On she went across the space, circled, and charged
back. Each time she went across the clearing she
slashed as a collie does in battle. Each time she
reached the shadow of the underbrush she wheeled and
came from a new direction.

Shouting his encouragement, Rowlie set to with
renewed vigor and began belaboring the two thieves.
He battered them about, driving them round the fire.
And the two found that no matter where they turned to
escape Rowlie, there was the tricolor animal that came,
always from a new direction, racing out of the
darkness, slashing with her keen fangs and away again
before they could strike at her.

Sometimes it seemed as though there must be two or
three dogs, for no matter which way the men turned
there was always one charging at them from a new direction.

They were helpless against such tactics. And at last,
harried and beaten, they attempted to retreat. It was
Snickers who went first, not thinking of his companion.
He fled in terror from the ghost that inflicted such
lance-wounds on his legs. He went crashing through
the brush in blind panic. And behind him, he soon
heard another crashing. It was Buckles, running blindly, anywhere, any direction, as long as it was away
from the foe that stuck so effectively and could not be
struck in return.

From the darkness behind him, Snickers could hear
a horrible, worrying sound. Then he heard the voice of
the pedlar.

"Come, come! Leave him alone, now. Not that he
doesn't deserve anything he gets, but I wouldn't have
ye kill him. Come!"

Snickers fled on. He was now alone and friendless.
He didn't want to meet Buckles, who would be sure to

accuse him of desertion in time of need—and he certainly had no more desire to meet the pedlar or his dog.

Snickers decided that he who traveled alone traveled fastest. He struck off to the west. And back by the campfire, Rowlie Palmer crouched beside a small white body. Lassie stood stiff-legged and touched it with her nose.

For a long time Rowlie crouched, unmoving, his mind crowded with the memories of many days when the little dog was his only companion.

At last he rose, went to the van and took out a spade. He began digging a small grave.

Lassie stood by the crossroads in the cold, driving rain. She whimpered once and saw the van stop. The man called to her. She shifted her feet in a sort of dance, but went no nearer. At last he walked back.

"Come here then, Your Majesty," he said.

She heard the first word and walked to the man who squatted on his heels on the muddy road. For a long time he patted and fondled her.

Then he rose.

"Won't ye come, then?" he asked.

Lassie lifted her head and moved her feet in the dance but still would not follow.

"Aye," he said. "Perhaps it's best that way. I'd like to go on with ye, but stock's low, and I've got to be getting back to Mark for the winter.

"And besides—ye'd never fit in with me like Toots did—and ye'd always be reminding me of her. Not that ye haven't been a good dog."

Lassie caught the last two words and moved her tail in acknowledgement.

"Aye, ye understand a lot, don't ye? Well, forgive

me—at first I thought ye were a coward, but it's not that. There's something else about thee, my lass, and I'd dearly love to be inside your mind and know what it is."

The collie heard the word "lass," and barked at it. The pedlar shook his head.

"Nay, that's the pity of it. Ye can understand some o' man's language, but man isn't bright enough to understand yours. And yet it's us that's supposed to be the most intelligent!

"Eigh, dear, but we had some good times going along the road together, didn't we? And now—if it's over, it's over. I'll be lonely. No thee—and no Toots. But I always did say if a man doesn't like to be alone, then he shouldn't never pick the job o' traveling pedlar for himself. It's what I must expect.

"And another way of looking at it. Sometimes I think ye didn't come along wi' me as much as ye let me come along with thee as long as our roads lay together. And now—well, ye'll be off about whatever business it is ye're on."

Lassie did not understand these words. All she knew was that the voice of the man who had fed and fondled her was a warm, soothing tone. So she nuzzled his hand.

"That's good-bye, eh?" he said. "Well, may luck go wi' thee, then. Off ye go!"

Lassie caught the word "go." She paced to the cross-road and turned away. There she looked back. The man waved.

"On ye go then, and good luck," he called.

He stood a long time watching the collie that trotted away. The cold afternoon rain beat in his weather-tanned face. He shook his head slowly, as if saying to himself that he would never be able to puzzle it out.

Soon the dog was lost from view. Rowlie went back to his van silently. He climbed aboard, clucked to Bess, and headed east.

Down on another road Lassie swung along—going south. The rain streamed from her coat; the mud splashed up over her legs.

A week later Rowlie's van moved slowly along the road. He did not sing now, nor did he walk beside his moving home, for the air was thick with flying white flakes.

Rowlie sat on the front seat, a tarpaulin buttoned over his knees, his buttony face bowed against the drive of the storm. The front of him was almost solid white, and before him he could see the steam rising from the flanks of Bess, as she plodded vigorously along.

"Aye, that's right," Rowlie said aloud. "Ye know we're almost home now. And glad I'll be to get there; for it's been a mucky trip back. Naught but rain, sleet, rain—and now snow. I stayed out too long on this trip—and that's what I get." Rowlie grumbled on, and then suddenly he stopped his lonesome talk. His mind went to the dog that had left him at the crossroads.

"Aye, well," he said finally. "I'm most home. And as for thee, my friend, here's hoping that whatever ye were seeking, ye've found it. Peace—or whatever it was ye were looking for. But wherever ye are—I hope ye're snug and warm and dry.

"Sometimes I wish I'd locked ye in the van and brought ye back wi' me; but I didn't have the heart to then—for I wanted no dog again after Toots. Perhaps I shall some day, but just now I don't. She were as true as they come—but happen ye're being true to something else. So good-bye to ye, and I hope ye're as near home as I am.

"There we are, Bess! Here's Twelve Corners. We'll be home i' time for tea wi' Mark."

As Bess plodded more vigorously and the van went toward home for the winter, many miles to the south Lassie plodded on.

Now she was crossing a great, high moor, where the wind swept without halt. The snowstorm drove from behind her, blowing the hair in sodden wisps forward from her thin flanks.

She found it hard to keep going. The snow was getting deeper, and it took more and more strength from her tired muscles to lift her feet clear of the snow at each step. At last she staggered and fell. Coiling up, she began biting the matted ice from the hair between her claws. Again she tried, but the snow was too deep. She began plunging at it like a horse, rearing and leaping forward, but before very long she found herself utterly exhausted.

She stood, her head down, the panted breath coming like white steam. She lifted her head and whined; but the snow was still there. She jumped and bucketed again, trying to leap through the drifts. Again she stopped, without power to go farther.

Then, lifting her head, she gave a long cry—the cry of a dog lost, cold, and helpless. It was a long, high call that went out over the wide moor, through the driving snow where the darkness was descending.

The snow blanketed all sounds. There was no one for miles on that flat, wild land. Even if there had been someone within a few hundred yards, it is doubtful whether or not he could have heard that snow-muffled cry.

At last Lassie sank to the ground. The white expanse of snow softly covered her. Below that white blanket she lay, exhausted but warm.

Journey's End

Sam Carraclough had spoken the truth early that year when he told his son Joe that it was a long way from Greenall Bridge in Yorkshire to the Duke of Rudling's place in Scotland. And it is just as many miles coming the other way, a matter of four hundred miles.

But that would be for a man traveling straight by road or by train. For an animal how far would it be— an animal that must circle and quest at obstacles, wander and err, backtrack and sidetrack till it found a way?

A thousand miles it would be—a thousand miles through strange terrain it had never crossed before, with nothing but instinct to tell direction.

Yes, a thousand miles of mountains and dale, of highland and moor, plowland and path, ravine and river and beck and burn; a thousand miles of tor and brae, of snow and rain and fog and sun; of wire and thistle and thorn and flint and rock to tear the feet— who could expect a dog to win through that?

Yet, if it were almost a miracle, in his heart Joe Carraclough tried to believe in that miracle—that somehow, wonderfully, inexplicably, his dog would be there some day; there, waiting by the school gate. Each day as he came out of school, his eyes would turn to the spot where Lassie had always waited. And each day there was nothing there, and Joe Carraclough would

walk home slowly, silently, stolidly as did the people of
his country.

Always, when school ended, Joe tried to prepare
himself—told himself not to be disappointed, because
there could be no dog there. Thus, through the long
weeks, Joe began to teach himself not to believe in the
impossible. He had hoped against hope so long that
hope began to die.

But if hope can die in a human it does not in an animal. As long as it lives, the hope is there and the faith
is there. And so, coming across the schoolyard that
day, Joe Carraclough would not believe his eyes. He
shook his head and blinked, and rubbed his fists in his
eyes, for he thought what he was seeing was a dream.
There, walking the last few yards to the school gate
was—his dog!

He stood, for the coming of the dog was terrible—
her walk was a thing that tore at her breath. Her head
and her tail were down almost to the pavement. Each
footstep forward seemed a separate effort. It was a
crawl rather than a walk. But the steps were made, one
by one, and at last the animal dropped in her place by
the gate and lay still.

Then Joe roused himself. Even if it were a dream, he
must do something. In dreams one must try.

He raced across the yard and fell to his knees, and
then, when his hands were touching and feeling fur, he
knew it was reality. His dog had come to meet him!

But what a dog was this—no prize collie with fine
tricolor coat glowing, with ears lifted gladly over the
proud slim head with its perfect black mask. It was not
a dog whose bright eyes were alert, and who jumped
up to bark a glad welcome. This was a dog that lay,
weakly trying to lift a head that would no longer lift;
trying to move a tail that was torn and matted with
thorns and burrs, and managing to do nothing very

much except to whine in a weak, happy, crying way. For she knew that at last the terrible driving instinct was at peace. She was at the place. She had kept her lifelong rendezvous, and hands were touching her that had not touched her for so long a time.

By the Labor Exchange, Ian Cawper stood with the other out-of-work miners, waiting until it was tea time so that they could all go back to their cottages.

You could have picked out Ian, for he was much the biggest man even among the many big men that Yorkshire grows. In fact, he was reputed to be the biggest and strongest man in all that Riding of Yorkshire. A big man, but gentle and often very slow of thinking and speech.

And so Ian was a few seconds behind the others in realizing that something of urgency was happening in the village. Then he too saw it—a boy struggling, half running, along the main street, his voice lifted in excitement, a great bundle of something in his arms.

The men stirred and moved forward. Then, when the boy was nearer, they heard his cry: "She's come back! She's come back!"

The men looked at each other and blew out their breath and then stared at the bundle the boy was carrying. It was true. Sam Carraclough's collie had walked back home from Scotland.

"I must get her home quick!" the boy was saying. He staggered on.

Ian Cawper stepped forward.

"Here," he said. "Run on ahead, tell 'em to get ready."

His great arms cradled the dog—arms that could have carried ten times the weight of this poor, thin animal.

"Oh, hurry, Ian!" the boy cried, dancing in excitement.

"I'm hurrying, lad. Go on ahead."

So Joe Carraclough raced along the street, turned up the side lane, ran down the garden path, and burst into the cottage: "Mother! Father!"

"What is it, lad?"

Joe paused. He could hardly get the words out—the excitement was choking up in his throat, hot and stifling. And then the words were said: "Lassie! She's come home! Lassie's come home!"

He opened the door, and Ian Cawper, bowing his head to pass under the lintel, carried the dog to the hearth and laid her there.

There were many things that Joe Carraclough was to remember from that evening. He was never to forget the look that passed over his father's face as he first knelt beside the dog that had been his for so many years, and let his hands travel over the emaciated frame. He was to remember how his mother moved about the kitchen, not grumbling or scolding now, but silently and with a sort of terrific intensity, poking the fire quickly, stirring the condensed milk into warm water, kneeling to hold the dog's head and lift open the jowl.

Not a word did his parents speak to him. They seemed to have forgotten him altogether. Instead, they both worked over the dog with a concentration that seemed to put them in a separate world.

Joe watched how his father spooned in the warm liquid, he saw how it drooled out again from the unswallowing dog's jowls and dribbled down onto the rug. He saw his mother warm up a blanket and wrap it round the dog. He saw them try again and again to feed her. He saw his father rise at last.

"It's no use, lass," he said to his mother.

Between his mother and father many questions and answers passed unspoken except through their eyes.

"Pneumonia," his father said at last. "She's not strong enough now . . ."

For a while his parents stood, and then it was his mother who seemed to be somehow wonderfully alive and strong.

"I won't be beat!" she said. "I just *won't* be beat."

She pursed her lips, and as if this grimace had settled something, she went to the mantlepiece and took down a vase. She turned it over and shook it. The copper pennies came into her hand. She held them out to her husband, not explaining nor needing to explain what was needed. But he stared at the money.

"Go on, lad," she said. "I were saving it for insurance, like."

"But how'll we . . ."

"Hush," the woman said.

Then her eyes flickered over her son, and Joe knew that they were aware of him again for the first time in an hour. His father looked at him, at the money in the woman's hand, and at last at the dog. Suddenly he took the money. He put on his cap and hurried out into the night. When he came back he was carrying bundles—eggs and a small bottle of brandy—precious and costly things in that home.

Joe watched as they were beaten together, and again and again his father tried to spoon some into the dog's mouth. Then his mother blew in exasperation. Angrily she snatched the spoon. She cradled the dog's head on her lap, she lifted the jowls, and poured and stroked the throat—stroked it and stroked it, until at last the dog swallowed.

"Aaaah!" It was his father, breathing a long, triumphant exclamation. And the firelight shone gold on his mother's hair as she crouched there, holding the dog's head—stroking its throat, soothing it with soft, loving sounds.

Joe did not clearly remember about it afterward, only a faint sensation that he was being carried to bed at some strange hour of darkness.

And in the morning when he rose, his father sat in his chair, but his mother was still on the rug, and the fire was still burning warm. The dog, swathed in blankets, lay quiet.

"Is she—dead?" Joe asked.

His mother smiled weakly.

"Shhh," she said. "She's just sleeping. And I suppose I ought to get breakfast—but I'm that played out—if I only had a nice strong cup o' tea . . ."

And that morning, strangely enough, it was his father who got the breakfast, boiling the water, brewing the tea, cutting the bread. It was his mother who sat in the rocking chair, waiting until it was ready.

That evening when Joe came home from school, Lassie still lay where he had left her when he went off to school. He wanted to sit and cradle her, but he knew that ill dogs are best left alone. All evening he sat, watching her, stretched out, with the faint breathing the only sign of life. He didn't want to go to bed.

"Now she'll be all right," his mother cried. "Go to bed—she'll be all right."

"Are you sure she'll get better, Mother?"

"Ye can see for yourself, can't ye? She doesn't look any worse, does she?"

"But are you sure she's going to be better?"

The woman sighed.

"Of course—I'm sure—now go to bed and sleep."

And Joe went to bed, confident in his parents.

That was one day. There were others to remember. There was the day when Joe returned and, as he walked to the hearth, there came from the dog lying there a movement that was meant to be a wag of the tail.

There was another day when Joe's mother sighed with pleasure, for as she prepared the bowl of milk, the dog stirred, lifted herself unsteadily, and waited. And when the bowl was set down, she put down her head and lapped, while her pinched flanks quivered.

And finally there was that day when Joe first realized that—even now—his dog was not to be his own again. So again the cottage rang with cries and protests, and again a woman's voice was lifted, tired and shrilling:

"Is there never to be any more peace and quiet in my home?"

And long after Joe had gone to bed, he heard the voices continuing—his mother's clear and rising and falling; his father's in a steady, reiterative monotone, never changing, always coming to one sentence: "But even if he would sell her back, where'd I get the brass to buy her—where's the money coming fro'? Ye know we can't get it."

To Joe Carraclough's father, life was laid out in straight rules. When a man could get work, he worked his best and got the best wage he could. If he raised a dog, he raised the best one he could. If he had a wife and children, he took care of them the best he could.

In this out-of-work collier's mind, there were no devious exceptions and evasions concerning life and its codes. Like most simple men, he saw all these things clearly. Lying, cheating, stealing—they were wrong, and you couldn't make them right by twisting them round in your mind.

So it was that, when he was faced with any problem, he so often brought it smack up against elemental truths.

"Honest is honest, and there's no two ways about it," he would say.

He had a habit of putting it like that. "Truth is truth." Or, "Cheating is cheating."

And the matter of Lassie came up against this simple, direct code of morals. He had sold the dog and taken the money and spent it. Therefore the dog did not belong to him any more, and no matter how you argued you could not change that. But a man has to live with his family, too. When a woman starts to argue with a man . . . well . . .

That next morning when Joe came down to breakfast, while his mother served the oatmeal with pursed lips, his father coughed and spoke as if he had rehearsed a set speech over in his mind many times that night:

"Joe, lad. We've decided upon it—that is, thy mother and me—that Lassie can stay here till she's all better.

"That's all right, because I believe true in ma heart that nobody could nurse her better and wi' more care nor we're doing. So that's honest. But when she's better, well . . .

"Now ye have her for a little while yet, so be content. And don't plague us, lad. There's enough things to worry us now wi'out more. So don't plague us no more—and try to be a man about it—and be content."

With the young, "for a little while" has two shapes. Seen from one end, it is a great, yawning stretch of time extending into the unlimitable future. From the other, it is a ghastly span of days that has been cruelly whisked away before the realization comes.

Joe Carraclough knew that it was the latter that morning when he went to school and heard a mighty, booming voice. As he turned to look, he saw in an automobile a fearsome old man and a girl with her flaxen hair cascading from under a beret. And the old man, with his ferocious white moustaches looking like an animal's misshapen fangs, was waving an ugly blackthorn stick to the danger of the car, the chauffeur, and the world in general, and shouting at him:

"Hi! Hi, there! Yes, I mean you, m' lad! Damme, Jenkins, will you make this smelly contraption stand still a moment? Whoa, there, Jenkins! Whoa! Why we ever stopped using horses is more than any sane man can understand. Country's going to pot, that's what! Here, m' lad! Come here!"

For a moment Joe thought of running—doing anything to get all these things he feared out of his sight, so that they might, miraculously, be out of his mind, too. But a machine can go faster than a boy, and then, too, Joe had in him the blood of men who might think slowly and stick to old ideas and bear trouble patiently—but who do not run away. So he stood sturdily on the pavement and remembered his manners as his mother had taught him, and said: "Yes, sir?"

"You're Whosis—What's-his-name's lad, aren't you?"

Joe's eyes had turned to the girl. She was the one he had seen long ago when he was putting Lassie in the Duke's kennels. Her face was not hearty-red like his own. It was blue-white. On the hand that clutched the edge of the car the veins stood out clear-blue. That hand looked thin. He was thinking that, as his mother would say, she could do with some plumduff.

She was looking at him, too. Something made him draw himself up proudly.

"My father is Sam Carraclough," he said firmly.

"I know, I know," the old man shouted impatiently. "I never forget a name. Never! Used to know every last soul in this village. Too many of you growing up now—younger generation. And, by gad, they're all of them not worth one of the old bunch—not the whole kit and caboodle. The modern generation, why . . ."

He halted, for the girl beside him was tugging his sleeve.

"What is it? Eh? Oh, yes. I was just coming to it. Where's your father, m' lad? Is he home?"

"No, sir."

"Where is he?"

"He's off over Allerby, sir."

"Allerby, what's he doing there?"

"A mate spoke for him at the pit, I think, and he's gone to see if there's a chance of getting taken on."

"Oh, yes—yes, of course. When'll he be back?"

"I don't know, sir. I think about tea."

"Don't mumble! Not till tea. Damme, very inconvenient—very! Well, I'll drop round about five-ish. You tell him to stay home and I want to see him—it's important. Tell him to wait."

Then the car was gone, and Joe hurried to school. There was never such a long morning as that one. The minutes in the classroom crawled past as the lessons droned on.

Joe had only one desire—to have it become noon. And when at last the leaden moments that were years were gone, he raced home and burst through the door. It was the same cry—for his mother.

"Mother, Mother!"

"Goodness, don't knock the door down. And close it—anyone would think you were brought up in a barn. What's the matter?"

"Mother, he's coming to take Lassie away!"

"Who is?"

"The Duke . . . he's coming . . ."

"The Duke? How in the world does he know that she's . . ."

"I don't know. But he stopped me this morning. He's coming at tea time . . ."

"Coming here? Are ye sure?"

"Yes, he said he'd come at tea. Oh, Mother, please . . ."

"Now, Joe. Don't start! Now I warn ye!"

"Mother, you've got to listen. Please, please!"

"You hear me? I said . . ."

"No, Mother. Please help me. Please!"

The woman looked at her son and heaved a sigh of weariness and exasperation. Then she threw up her hands in despair. "Eigh, dearie me! Is there never to be any more peace in this house? Never?"

She sank into her chair and looked at the floor. The boy went to her and touched her arm.

"Mother—do something," the boy pleaded. "Can't we hide her? He'll be here at five. He told me to tell Father he'd be here at five. Oh, Mother . . ."

"Nay, Joe. Thy father won't . . ."

"Won't you beg him? Please, please! Beg Father to . . ."

"Joe!" his mother cried angrily. Then her voice became patient again. "Now, Joe, it's no use. So stop thy plaguing. It's just that thy father won't lie. That much I'll give him. Come good, come bad, he'll not lie."

"But just this once, Mother."

The woman shook her head sadly and sat by the fire, staring into it as if she would find peace there. Her son went to her and touched her bare forearm.

"Please, Mother. Beg him. Just this once. Just one lie wouldn't hurt him. I'll make it up to him, I will. I will, truly!"

The words began to race from his mouth quickly.

"I'll make it up to both of you. When I'm growed up, I'll get a job. I'll earn money. I'll buy him things— I'll buy you things, too. I'll buy you both anything you ever want, if you'll only please, please . . ."

And then, for the first time in all his trouble, Joe

Carraclough became a child, his sturdiness gone, and the tears choked his voice. His mother could hear his sobs, and she patted his hand, but she would not look at him. From the magic of the fire she seemed to read deep wisdom, and she spoke slowly.

"Tha mustn't, Joe," she said, her words soft. "Tha mustn't want like that. Tha must learn never to want anything i' life so hard as tha wants Lassie. It doesn't do."

It was then that she felt her son's hand trembling with impatience, and his voice rising clear.

"Ye don't understand, Mother. Ye don't understand. It ain't me that wants her. It's her that wants us—so terrible bad. That's what made her come home all that way. She wants us, so terrible bad."

It was then that Mrs. Carraclough looked at her son at last. She could see his face, contorted, and the tears rolling openly down his cheeks. And yet, in that moment of childishness, it was as if he were suddenly all the more grown up. Mrs. Carraclough felt as if time had jumped, and she were seeing this boy, this son of her own, for the first time in many years.

She stared at him and then she clasped her hands together. Her lips pressed together in a straight light and she got up.

"Joe, come and eat, then. And go back to school and be content. I'll talk to thy father."

She lifted her head, and her voice sounded firm.

"Yes—I'll talk to him, all right. I'll talk to Mr. Samuel Carraclough. I will indeed!"

At five that afternoon, the Duke of Rudling, fuming and muttering in his bad-tempered way, got out of a car that had stopped by a cottage gate. And behind the gate was a boy, who stood sturdily, his feet apart, as if to bar the way.

"Well, well, m' lad! Did ye tell him?"

"Go away," the boy said fiercely. "Go away! Thy tyke's net here."

For once in his life the Duke of Rudling stepped backward. He stared at the boy in amazement.

"Well, drat my buttons, Priscilla," he breathed. "Th' lad's touched. He is—he's touched!"

"Thy tyke's net here. Away wi' thee," the boy said stoutly. And it seemed as if in his determination he spoke in the broadest dialect he could command.

"What's he saying?" Priscilla asked.

"He's saying my dog isn't here. Drat my buttons, are you going deaf, Priscilla? I'm supposed to be deaf, and I can hear him all right. Now, ma lad, what tyke o' mine's net here?"

The Duke, when he answered, also turned to the broadest tones of Yorkshire dialect, as he always did to the people of the cottages—a habit which many of the members of the Duke's family deplored deeply.

"Coom, coom, ma lad. Speak up! What tyke's net here?"

As he spoke he waved his cane ferociously and advanced. Joe Carraclough stepped back from the fearful old man, but he still barred the path.

"No tyke o' thine," he cried stoutly.

But the Duke continued to advance. The words raced from Joe's mouth with a torrent of despair.

"Us hasn't got her. She's not here. She couldn't be here. No tyke could ha' done it. No tyke could come all them miles. It's not Lassie—it's—it's just another one that looks like her. It isn't Lassie."

"Well, bless my heart and soul," puffed the Duke. "Bless my heart and soul. Where's thy father, lad?"

Joe shook his head grimly. But behind him the cottage door opened and his mother's voice spoke.

"If it's Sam Carraclough ye're looking for—he's out in the shed, and been shut up there half the afternoon."

"What's this lad talking about—a dog o' mine being here?"

"Nay, ye're mistaken," the woman said stoutly.

"I'm mistaken?" roared the Duke.

"Yes. He didn't say a tyke o' thine was here. He said it wasn't here."

"Drat my buttons," the Duke sputtered angrily. "Don't twist my words up."

Then his eyes narrowed, and he stepped a pace forward.

"Well, if he said a dog of mine *isn't*, perhaps you'll be good enough to tell me just *which* dog of mine it is that isn't here. Now," he finished triumphantly. "Come, come! Answer me!"

Joe, watching his mother, saw her swallow and then look about her as if for help. She pressed her lips together. The Duke stood waiting for his answer, peering out angrily from beneath his jutting eyebrows. Then Mrs. Carraclough drew a breath to speak.

But her answer, truth or lie, was never spoken. For they all heard the rattle of a chain being drawn from a door, and then the voice of Sam Carraclough said clearly:

"This, I give ye my word, is th' only tyke us has here. So tell me, does it look like any dog that belongs to thee?"

Joe's mouth was opening for a last cry of protest, but as his eyes fell on the dog by his father, the exclamation died. And he stared in amazement.

There he saw his father, Sam Carraclough, the collie fancier, standing with a dog at his heels the like of which few men had ever seen before, or would wish to see. It was a dog that sat patiently at his left heel, as any well-trained dog should do—just as Lassie used to do. But this dog—it was ridiculous to think of it at the same moment as Lassie.

For where Lassie's skull was aristocratic and slim, this dog's head was clumsy and rough. Where Lassie's ears stood in the grace of twin-lapped symmetry, this dog had one screw ear and the other standing up Alsatian fashion, in a way that would give any collie breeder the cold shivers.

More than that. Where Lassie's coat faded to delicate sable, this curious dog had ugly splashes of black; and where Lassie's apron was a billowing expanse of white, this dog had muddy puddles of off-color, blue-merle mixture. Lassie had four white paws, and this one had only one white, two dirty-brown, and one almost black. Lassie's tail flowed gracefully behind her, and this dog's tail looked like something added as an afterthought.

And yet, as Joe Carraclough looked at the dog beside his father, he understood. He knew that if a dog coper could treat a dog with cunning so that its bad points came to look like good ones, he could also reverse the process and make all its good ones look like bad ones—especially if that man were his father, one of the most knowing of dog fanciers in all that Riding of Yorkshire.

In that moment, he understood his father's words, too. For in dog-dealing, as in horse-dealing, the spoken word is a binding contract, and once it is given, no real dog-man will attempt to go back on it.

And that was how his father, in his patient, slow way, had tried to escape with honor. He had not lied. He had not denied anything. He had merely asked a question:

"Tell me, does this dog look like any dog that belongs to thee?"

And the Duke had only to say:

"Why, that's not my dog," and forever after, it would not be his.

So the boy, his mother and his father, gazed steadily at the old man, and waited with held breath as he continued to stare at the dog.

But the Duke of Rudling knew many things too—many, many things. And he was not answering. Instead he was walking forward slowly, the great cane now tapping as he leaned on it. His eyes never left the dog for a second. Slowly, as if he were in a dream, he knelt down, and his hand made one gentle movement. It picked up a forepaw and turned it slightly. So he knelt by the collie, looking with eyes that were as knowing about dogs as any man in Yorkshire. And those eyes did not waste themselves upon twisted ears or blotched markings or rough head. Instead, they stared steadily at the underside of the paw, seeing only the five black pads, crossed and recrossed with half-healed scars where thorns had torn and stones had lacerated.

Then the Duke lifted his head, but for a long time he knelt, gazing into space, while they waited. When he did get up, he spoke, not using Yorkshire dialect any more, but speaking as one gentleman might address another.

"Sam Carraclough," he said. "This is no dog of mine. 'Pon my soul and honor, she never belonged to me. No! Not for a single second did she ever belong to me!"

Then he turned and walked down the path, thumping his cane and muttering: "Bless my soul! I wouldn't ha' believed it! Bless my soul! Four hundred miles! I wouldn't ha' believed it."

It was at the gate that his granddaughter tugged his sleeve.

"What you came for," she whispered. "Remember?"

The Duke seemed to come from his dream, and then he suddenly turned into his old self again.

"Don't whisper! What's that? Oh, yes, of course.

You don't need to tell me—I hadn't forgotten!"

He turned and made his voice terrible.

"Carraclough! Carraclough! Drat my buttons, where are ye? What're ye hiding for?"

"I'm still here, sir."

"Oh, yes. Yes. Of course. There you are. You working?"

"Eigh, now—working," Joe's father said. That was the best he could manage.

"Yes, working—working! A job! A job! Do you have one?" the Duke fumed.

"Well, now—it's this road . . ." began Carraclough.

As he fumbled his words, Mrs. Carraclough came to his rescue, as good housewives will in Yorkshire—and in most other parts of the world.

"My Sam's not exactly working, but he's got three or four things that he's been considering. Sort of investigating, as ye might say. But—he hasn't quite said yes or no to any of them yet."

"Then he'd better say no, and quickly," snapped the Duke. "I need somebody up at my kennels. And I think, Carraclough . . ." His eyes turned to the dog still sitting at the man's heel. ". . . I think you must know—a lot—about dogs. So there. That's settled."

"Nay, hold on," Carraclough said. "Ye see, I wouldn't like to think I got a chap into trouble and then took his job. Ye see, Mr. Hynes couldn't help . . ."

"Hynes!" snorted the Duke. "Hynes! Utter nincompoop. Had to sack him. Didn't know a dog from a ringtailed filly. Should ha' known no Londoner could ever run a kennel for a Yorkshireman's taste. Now, I want you for the job."

"Nay, there's still something," Mrs. Carraclough protested.

"What now?"

"Well, how much would this position be paying?"

The Duke puffed his lips.

"How much do you want, Carraclough?"

"Seven pounds a week, and worth every penny," Mrs. Carraclough cut in, before her husband could even get round to drawing a preparatory breath.

But the Duke was a Yorkshireman, too, and that meant he would scorn himself if he missed a chance to be "practical," as they say, where money is concerned.

"Five," he roared. "And not a penny more."

"Six pounds, ten," bargained Mrs. Carraclough.

"Six even," offered the Duke cannily.

"Done," said Mrs. Carraclough, as quick as a hawk's swoop.

They both glowed, self-righteously pleased with themselves. Mrs. Carraclough would have been willing to settle for three pounds a week in the first place— and as for the Duke, he felt he was getting a man for his kennels who was beyond price.

"Then it's settled," the Duke said.

"Well, almost," the woman said. "I presume, of course . . ." She liked the taste of what she considered a very fine word, so she repeated it. ". . . I presume that means we get the cottage on the estate, too."

"Ye drive a fierce bargain, ma'am," said the Duke, scowling. "But ye get it—on one condition." He lifted his voice and roared. "On condition that as long as ye live on my land, you never allow that thick-skulled, screw-lugged, gay-tailed eyesore of an excuse for a collie on my property. Now, what do ye say?"

He waited, rumbling and chuckling happily to himself as Sam Carraclough stooped, perplexed. But it was the boy who answered gladly: "Oh, no, sir. She'll be down at school waiting for me most o' the time. And, anyway, in a day or so we'll have her fixed up so's ye'd never recognize her."

"I don't doubt that," puffed the Duke, as he stumped toward his car. "I don't doubt ye could do exactly that. Hmm . . . Well, I never . . ."

It was afterward in the car that the girl edged close to the old man.

"Now don't wriggle," he protested. "I can't stand anyone wriggling."

"Grandfather," she said. "You are kind—I mean about their dog."

The old man coughed and cleared his throat.

"Nonsense," he growled. "Nonsense. When you grow up, you'll understand that I'm what people call a hard-hearted Yorkshire realist. For five years I've sworn I'd have that dog. And now I've got her."

Then he shook his head slowly.

"But I had to buy the man to get her. Ah, well. Perhaps that's not the worst part of the bargain."

Just Like Old Times Again

When young Joe Carraclough said that you wouldn't have recognized his dog in a few days, he was right or wrong, according to what you thought his dog ought to look like. Certainly, if you had looked for the screw-eared, gay-tailed horror that his father had coped up in his simple attempt to have the dog for his son and yet not trespass upon his stern codes of honesty, you would have never recognized it. But if you had looked for that proud, graceful, slim-headed dog known as Sam Carraclough's Lassie, you would have found her.

There she was, and as the weeks passed, under careful feeding and correct treatment, she slowly blossomed back into the dog she had once been. The gauntness and the pinched flanks disappeared, and the years of proper care that had built a strong constitution aided her now. Once more the rich coat billowed in black-white- and golden-sable making her a delight to the eye. There was left only a slight limp where the bullet had creased her flank. The muscles had stiffened and, try as Sam Carraclough would, even with all his secrets and magics, he could never quite cure that.

But he did well with it, and massaged and rubbed the dog's muscles until the limp was so slight that only a dog expert would have noticed the tiny "favoring" of that foot as the dog went along. To the eye of all except the most expert dog-man, she would have been that most beautiful thing—a perfect collie.

And each weekday, a few minutes before four o'clock, once again the shopkeepers of Greenall Bridge would look out and see that proud dog going down the street, and say, "You can set your clocks by her." And always, a few minutes later Joe Carraclough would come out of school and greet his dog, and they would go home together happily.

Yet, when young Joe promised the Duke that the dog would always be waiting for him, he was wrong there, too. For there came a time when Lassie appeared no more at the school gate. Strangely enough, however, Joe didn't seem to care. He seemed perfectly happy, with a sort of secret happiness, as he went home alone.

It was one of those days that, as he went along the gravel path of the Duke's grounds whistling to himself, he saw the girl again.

Somehow Joe felt sorry for her. She did not look nice and plump and solid-boned as the little girls of the village did.

"Hello," he said.

"Hello," she answered.

There seemed nothing else to say, but he stood there.

"I've been away at school," she said.

"Have you?"

"Yes. But it's holidays now."

He thought gravely about that. "We don't have our holidays for another week," he announced.

There was another pause, and then she said: "How is Lassie?"

Joe smiled his warm smile. He looked around, as if to make sure no one was listening.

"You can come and see," he said, as if conferring a favor.

He led the way down the path to the cottage where the hollyhocks, gay-colored and tall, grew beside the white wall. He opened the door.

"Mother," he said. "I'm going to show her."

"Why, do come in, Miss," his mother said, smoothing her apron and then wiping an imaginary piece of dust from the white tablecloth set for tea.

Joe led the way to the cool scullery, where a great, low box was set in the dimness. And in the box was Lassie, and piled about her were seven plump, sleeping balls of fur.

"You see," Joe explained proudly, "we keep her here because she'd fret in the kennels. That's because she's a home dog, Lassie is."

The girl crouched down and touched one ball of fur with her forefinger. The little thing gave a drunken hiccup.

"Are they still blind?" she asked, as they both laughed.

Joe expanded.

"Of course not. Why, they get their eyes open when they're ten days old. These are over three weeks old now. They can run—only they like to sleep most of the time it seems to me."

He smiled as Lassie lifted her head. He stroked it gently.

"You know a lot about them, don't you?" the girl asked humbly.

"Well, she had a litter once before," Joe disclaimed, "and I remember from that time. This is just like old times—isn't it, Lassie?"

He crouched there, looking at his dog. It was like old times. He had often thought about that of late.

After the girl had gone, and polite good-byes and invitations to come and see the puppies again had been issued, Joe was still thinking about that. It was almost as if he was going to discover some sort of answer about life that, as a boy, he had never reached before.

This was like old times. Although, of course, it was a different house that they lived in now, it was as it used to be a year or so ago—in so many ways.

For example, if he took an extra big spoonful of sugar on his oatmeal in the morning, no longer did his mother snap at him and say:

"Now be careful, young man! Sugar costs money!"

Or, if he came in from the raw Yorkshire air boasting of how hungry he was, no longer did his mother's face take on that frightened, secret look, but instead she would laugh in her merry, plump way and say:

"My goodness, I don't know how to keep ye full! Where do ye put it all?"

But all the time she was saying it, her voice would sound as if she were proud of a son who had such a great appetite, and that was just as it used to be in old times, too.

No longer did the grownups stop talking when he came in suddenly, nor did the voices go on, lifting and falling in weary argument after he was abed. No longer did his father come home each day, weary and dour and unspeaking, to sit by the fire and gaze into it.

Instead, the moment his footstep would sound out on the gravel, Mrs. Carraclough would jump up in a great bustle and cry:

"Look out! Here comes thy father now! Heads up—hot stuff coming!"

Then she would race from fire to table, whisking steaming tureens and bowls from the oven as if the most important thing in all the world was that they should all be set out in that brief space of time between the sound of his coming and the opening of the door.

Then she would stand, her arms akimbo, and say:

"Hurry up and wash, Sam! Sheep's head and

dumplings tonight—and they don't wait for no man!

That was the way it was—like old times again. And his father, too, sitting at the table, bowing his head to the food and then looking up and saying:

"Well, and how's our Joe been today? Did ye do your lessons good at school?"

Once it had been like that before. Then it had all stopped. Now it was like that again. What was the reason?

Joe pondered over this all through the meal that evening. After the meal was over, and Lassie came stalking in, he sank on the rug beside her and stroked her, and he thought he had found the answer.

It was Lassie! Of course—that was it! When she had been home, things had been right. When she was sold and gone, nothing had gone right any more. And now that she was back, everything was fine again, and they were all very happy.

"She came home and brought us luck," he thought. "She did it. She came home and brought us luck."

He made a crooning sound and pillowed his face in the dog's ruff. Lassie sighed contentedly.

Then his mother spoke:

"Now Joe, don't lie with that dog all over my rug. Getting hair all over. And what's making you so silent tonight?"

Joe smiled to himself. He still crooned to the dog.

"Ye're a come-home dog, aren't ye, Lassie?" he crooned. "Aye, that ye are. And ye brought us luck. 'Cause ye're a come-homer. Ye're my Lassie Come-home. That's thy name! Lassie Come-home!"

But his mother stormed again.

"Did ye hear me, Joe Carraclough? Now tha'll have her all upset—and when she's got a litter to take care on. Tha should know better nor that!"

Joe edged an inch away from the fire and stroked

the contented Lassie. He looked up gravely.

"Eigh, Feyther," he said, "I can feel her ribs."

His father turned his chair to the hearth and stretched his legs luxuriously, and then began lighting his pipe, smiling to himself.

"Don't ye think she's a bit poor, Feyther?" Joe went on anxiously. "I think she could stand a little more beef and a little less milk!"

"Ah, ye do, do ye?" his mother chattered on, as she piled up the steaming dishes she was washing. "Is that so? Ye think she could stand more beef. Aye, well, tha wouldn't be a Carraclough—nor a Yorkshireman—if tha didn't think tha knew more about raising tykes nor breaking eggs wi' a stick!

"Aye—sometimes it seems to me that some folk in this village think more o' their tykes nor they do o' their own flesh and blood. Dogs, dogs, dogs—After this litter's raised, out she goes where she belongs, and never another dog will I have in my home . . ."

Just then Joe looked up at his father, who was looking down out of the side of his eyes. And his father lifted his hand and put his finger comically beside his nose.

That secret gesture had a meaning. It meant:

"Ye mustn't mind women too much, Joe. They have a hard time of it, staying home and scrubbing and scouring and cooking all day, and so they take it out in scolding, and we've got to let them do it to blow off steam. But we know it doesn't really mean anything, we men know that—we men!"

And his father smiled, and Joe grinned, and then it was so funny, this new kinship of men that let women go on scolding, that Joe started to laugh. His laughter rose and rose, until his mother turned.

"Aye, and now ye laugh at me, do ye! Well, I'll teach ye! I'll give ye a skelp!"

And she flicked him with the dishtowel expertly, till Joe rolled over.

"I wasn't laughing at you, Mother!"

"Well, what were ye laughing at?"

"At Father—he made a funny face!"

Mrs. Carraclough turned on her husband.

"So it were thee, eh? Well, I'll skelp thee, too!"

But as she advanced, Joe saw his father's great strong hands reach out, and one of them imprisoned his mother's shining wrists and the other arm went around her great waist, and Mrs. Carraclough was held fast. Then the father looked at Joe and smiled: "Look at her, Joe. Who's the bonniest woman in the whole village?"

"My mother is," Joe said stoutly and with all the honesty in his heart.

Mrs. Carraclough's face broke into a beam.

"The two of ye," she said. "Ah, ye're both chips off the same stick. Ye're both saying that to blarney me."

"Nay, the lad answered an honest question honestly. And another thing—tha's bonnie—and there's plenty of thee, too!"

"Oh, so tha thinks I'm plump. Well, let me go, Sam Carraclough. I've got to finish drying them dishes!"

But his father wouldn't let his mother go, and she began boxing his ears, and he just sat there with his head bowed to protect his pipe. Then they both laughed.

That was just as it used to be long ago, too—his father and mother happy.

Joe bowed his head to the dog, and forgot them.

"You're my Lassie Come-home," he crooned.

About the Author

Eric Knight, born in 1897 to Quaker parents, was a Yorkshire lad. His father died when Eric was still quite young and soon after, his mother went to Russia to become governess to Princess Xenia's children. Eric remained in England, living in the West Riding of Yorkshire with his Aunt Kit and learning at first hand the life of the villages and the moors beyond. When hard times came to the community, Eric held his first job at the age of thirteen.

By 1912, Eric's mother had remarried and was living in the United States. When Eric joined her in Philadelphia, he continued to hold jobs, the first of which was as copy-boy on a city newspaper. He also managed to attend the Cambridge Latin School in Massachusetts and the Boston Academy of Fine Arts. World War I, and his allegiance to his native land, prompted him to go to Canada and enlist in the famous Princess Pat's Regiment.

After the war, Eric Knight turned to a career as a newspaperman. His success as the film critic for the Philadelphia *Public Ledger* led him to a brief period of screen-writing in Hollywood. By 1935, however, he was working full time on his own novels and short stories, one of which won a place in the O'Henry Memorial Collection of prize stories. Others of his stories received honors including "The Flying Yorkshireman"

which became the title story of the Book-of-the-Month
Club selection. This and his Sam Small Stories, like
LASSIE COME-HOME, were notable for their use of
Yorkshire dialect.

In 1939, Eric Knight, his wife Jere and their collie,
settled on a farm in Pennsylvania. There, among the
hills so reminiscent of the north of England, LASSIE
COME-HOME was written. In 1941 his celebrated adult
novel *This Above All* was published and soon after
Knight and his wife went to England on behalf of the
British Ministry of Information to aid British-Ameri-
can relations. After their return in 1942, Eric Knight
was commissioned in the American army. He died in a
plane crash over Dutch Guiana en route to Africa in
January of 1943.

About the Book

LASSIE COME-HOME was first published as a short story in the *Saturday Evening Post* magazine. Its immense popularity led an editor at the John C. Winston Company to believe that it should be published as a book. He asked Eric Knight if the story could be lengthened and found that LASSIE originally had been shortened for magazine publication, so it was not difficult to restore the ommitted parts and to add new adventures to the saga of the come-home dog.

Over the years since the story was first published, many young people have written the author to ask how he happened to write it. Did he actually own a come-home dog? Yes he did. From 1934 until his death, Knight had owned a beautiful and highly intelligent collie named "Toots." Even before that time, Knight had raised collies on his Pennsylvania farm, and as a boy he had often heard his Uncle Ned tell tales of another, earlier come-home collie. Thus, it was natural for the writer to recreate this story and to set it against the background of his childhood. He had known the poverty of the Yorkshire people and understood their pride and stubbornness. There is scarcely an anthology of dog stories published in the United States, Canada and British Commonwealth that does not include a portion of the original LASSIE story.

The book LASSIE COME-HOME was published in

1940 and had an immediate success. It was recommend-
ed by the Book-of-the-Month Club in the United
States; then they reprinted it in Canada as a special edition illustrated by Cyrus Baldridge. Altogether, in the
various English language editions, LASSIE COME-HOME
has now sold well over a million copies.

The book is dedicated to the late Dr. Henry Jarrett,
a notable veterinary doctor, who introduced the first
collies into the United States early in this century. An
Englishman by birth, he formed a special friendship
with Eric Knight.

The book was made into a notable film by Metro-
Goldwyn-Mayer in 1942, a motion picture, inciden-
tally, that delighted the author. The television series
entitled LASSIE stems from the original motion picture
and has been almost as long-lived as the book. Now a
classic of its kind, LASSIE COME-HOME has been published and republished all over the world in twenty-
four foreign languages. It is, for example, required
reading in the schools of Poland.

This new American edition contains some changes
that the author had planned before his death. It cel-
ebrates the third decade in the life of the book.